A Collection of Short Horror Stories

by S.E. Howard

Copyright 2025 S.E. Howard

Cover art by Ruth Anna Evans Cover Designs

Interior art for "Beware the Grindlewog" by Sloane Reinke

Names, characters and incidents depicted in this book are products of the author's imagination or are used fictitiously. Any resemblance to actual events, locales, organizations or persons, living or dead, is entirely coincidental and beyond the intent of the author. No part of this book may be reproduced or transmitted in any form or by any means, electronic or mechanical, including photocopying, recording or by any information storage or retrieval system without permission in writing from the author.

S.E. Howard

Table of Contents

The Bobbit 4

Swan Song 10

The Stranger 36

The Baxter Family's Quantum Vacation 54

Beware The Grindlewog 91

The Devil You Know 104

What Fresh Hell Is This? 123

Just Deserts 144

It Will Have Blood 156

You've Been Saved 181

The Periphery People 204

About The Author 215

Acknowledgements 216

The Bobbit

"Mommy, there's a bobbit in the yard," Jack cried, rushing into the kitchen and leaving a trail of splattered blood on the floor.

Elaine Crosby turned, her hands submerged in a suds-filled sink of dirty dishes. "Jonathan Michael Crosby," she scolded. "Look at the mess you've made!"

"But, Mommy," the boy gulped. "There's a bobbit!"

"It ate Petie!" wailed Norah, bursting through the back door behind her brother. "Oh, Mommy, it's hiding by the rose bushes, and it swallowed poor Petie right up!"

Petie was the family's dog. No bigger than a loaf of bread, it remained nonetheless convinced that it was somehow instead the size of a Great Pyrenees and defended the virtues of the entire Crosby clan accordingly. Moments earlier, Elaine had heard it barking outside but assumed yet again it had caught sight of Mr. Willoughby, their nosy next-door neighbor. Now, however, as she took in the looks of undisguised horror on her children's faces, along with the gore splattered on their legs, she realized she'd been mistaken.

"Oh, dear," she said, reaching behind her to untie her apron strings. "Show me where."

While Norah stood trembling by the stoop, Jack led Elaine to the edge of the patio. With a shaking finger, he pointed out the back corner of the yard. "O-over there."

"How big was it?"

"I don't know. I couldn't see much of it. Just its jaws when they swung shut." He looked up at his mother, ashen with fright. "Do you think it's the same one that ate Mrs. Ferguson?"

"Darling, don't be silly. That happened months ago. Practically last year."

"But they never found it," Jack whispered, all round and frightened eyes. "The Agency dug out its tunnel, remember? They never found it."

The Agency couldn't find its own ass with both hands, a map, and a week to try, Elaine thought. "I'm sure it's not the same one," she reassured her son. "Now be a lamb, won't you, and run into the garage? Bring me the shovel. The big one, not the hand trowel."

She watched him hurry toward the garage, being sure to keep to the paved walking path and driveway. This was the third time they'd come across a bobbit in at least as many months, and she worried the poor boy would never step foot in the grass again out of sheer terror.

"Mommy," Norah whined from behind her. "Should I call the Agency?"

"Yes, please." Elaine turned to the girl, her mouth stretched in a smile. "That would be lovely. Thank you."

Norah nodded, then ran inside once more. Seconds later, Jack returned, carrying the shovel, and wearing a gas mask. Reaching into the pocket of his shirt, he pulled out a pair of goggles. "I got these for you, too."

"Thank you, Jack. That's very thoughtful." Elaine slipped the elastic band behind her head, then drew the goggles up to rest against the bridge of her nose. "Your sister's gone inside to call the Agency. You stay here while I go take a look-see-loo."

Nobody could say for sure when bobbits first made the transition from the ocean floor to dry land. Some scientists speculated that the deaths of coral reefs, brought about by climate change, had driven away the fish they historically preyed upon. Compared to the slim pickings found in the bleached, abandoned ruins of the reefs, the back yards, playgrounds, and public parks of suburbia must have seemed like all-you-can-eat bonanzas.

She'd read that the worms could reach up to ten feet in length in their native environments. Their prospective prey on land was significantly larger, however, and the bobbits had accommodated for this by increasing in size. The Agency estimated that the bobbit that had killed poor Mrs. Ferguson, the kindly old woman who'd lived three doors down, had been anywhere from thirty-five to forty feet long, with a bite radius of at least eleven feet. They'd found the top of Mrs. Ferguson's head—that's all, just the bloody cap of her skull with some brain matter still affixed. The rest of her, it seemed, had been gobbled up whole.

As she neared the corner of the yard, Elaine caught sight of it, camouflaged as it lay hidden in the lawn. Its tentacles splayed out around its head in a wide corona, while its serrated jaws lay open like a bear trap waiting to be triggered. She stopped within a foot of the worm, close enough so that it sensed the vibrations of her footsteps. Its tentacles twitched in her direction, mimicking the movement of grass blades in a breeze, but Elaine wasn't fooled.

"Mommy," she heard Norah say, followed by the slap of the back door as it shut behind her. "I called the Agency."

"Thank you," Elaine said, glancing back at the children. "You and Jack wait there while I—"

A sudden blur of movement out of the corner of her eye made her whirl back around, just as the bobbit leaped from the vertical shaft into which it had burrowed, springing in attack.

"*Mommy!*" Jack and Norah wailed together.

Elaine swung the shovel like a baseball bat, and the metal head smashed into the worm, knocking it sideways. Its pincher-like jaws slammed together within centimeters of her face, then it crashed to the ground. Before it could recover and come at her again, she drove the point of the spade down into its head. Gritting her teeth, she leaped onto the shovel blade like she might have a pogo stick, bearing all of her weight down as she punched through the other side of the bobbit's head, impaling it against the ground.

The bobbit thrashed, its long body whipping back and forth, the tentacles framing its mouth flailing wildly, desperately. Blood sprayed in all directions, splattering across the front of Elaine's blouse and skirt, splashing her face and goggles. Only when at last, the worm fell still did she release the shovel and stumble away. She'd lost one of her shoes somehow, ripped her skirt up the back, and popped at least three buttons off her shirt in the struggle.

"Mommy!" Jack rushed across the yard, braving the grass to crash into her, clinging to her waist.

"Hush now," Elaine said, gore dripping from her hair. "It's alright."

Norah raced toward her, too, and she held them both, one tucked against each hip. When she looked up, she found her neighbor, Mr. Willoughby, watching from his own yard next door. A garden hose dangled limply from his hand, water dribbling out.

"Everything alright?" he called.

"Everything's fine," she replied. "Just clearing out a bobbit."

"Another one? Do you need me to call the Agency?"

"Already taken care of but thank you." Turning the kids around, she ushered them toward the back door. "Come on now, back inside, the both of you. Jack, take that gas mask off this instant. Let's get cleaned up before your father gets home."

Shaking his head, Mr. Willoughby turned his hose back up, spraying his hydrangeas. "Goddamn bobbits," he muttered.

Swan Song

"There are things known and there are things unknown, and in between are the doors." – Aldous Huxley

"Daddy, are you coming home?"

Paul Santino suppressed an outward wince at the eager hope in his daughter, Lucy's voice. "Not today, punkin. Not for awhile yet. Daddy's working, remember?"

Through Facetime, he watched Lucy's mouth scrunch into a puzzled sort of frown. "Mommy said they weren't going to make your movie anymore. They had to stop because people got sick."

Your movie. He had to smile at Lucy's naivete.

He used to have dreams of becoming a movie star. Now he just hoped to land enough acting gigs to keep the bills paid. He'd built a mediocre living over the past 10 years doing bit parts, commercial roles, corporate voice-overs, and cheesy B-grade horror movies.

Including this one, he thought, because in terms of his career, *Hotel Evil: The Movie* was pretty much the equivalent of hitting rock bottom. At terminal velocity.

"They stopped for a little while," he tried to explain to Lucy. "Not forever."

Production had been halted because of COVID-19, leaving Paul and most of the cast and crew stranded at their shooting location, the Piedmont Hotel, in the middle of godforsaken nowhere.

"It's only temporary," Jason Horn, the director, had assured them. "We'll be underway again in no time, so just sit back, relax, and be patient."

Easy for him to say, Paul figured, considering the son of a bitch lived close enough to the Piedmont, he'd been able to quarantine from the cozy comfort of home.

And he doesn't have a wife who's constantly on his ass.

"Mommy wants to talk to you," Lucy said.

Speak of the devil, Paul thought. "Sure thing, punkin," he said, walking into the bathroom and snapping on the lights. "How about a kiss first?"

She smooshed her puckered lips against the phone screen. "I love you, Daddy!"

He made silly kissing sounds that left her giggling. "I love you, too. It's bedtime there. Go brush your teeth."

"Brush *your* teeth!" she exclaimed.

He'd come to stand before the vanity sink and reached down into his toiletry bag on the counter. Producing a toothbrush from inside, he held it up with a dramatic flourish, like a magician showing off his wand.

"I bet I'm done before you are," he said, and now Lucy squealed with laughter.

"Nuh-uh!" she cried, and the view careened wildly toward the ceiling on her end of things as she dropped the phone and scampered off toward the bathroom.

Seconds later, the view shifted again as his wife, Julia, picked the phone up.

"Hey, babe," Paul said, trying to affect good cheer.

He wasn't now, nor had he ever been, that great an actor.

"Have you heard from Horn yet?" she asked with no preamble or pretense.

"Not yet. He said to be patient."

"They're saying on the news that people should plan on quarantining themselves for six weeks or more."

"It's a production delay," he assured her. "That's all. It happens all the time for different reasons."

"Yes, but you're not getting paid in the meantime," she argued. "And you're stuck out there when you could be back here, going to auditions or booking jobs—"

"Julia," he interjected patiently. "We've talked about this. I signed a contract. I can't back out of it now."

Primarily because *Hotel Evil* had paid upfront, and the money was already spent. The drawback to being a starving actor, Paul had discovered over the years, was the *starving* part. Living in California wasn't cheap. Neither was health insurance.

"I still think you should talk to Margie—" she began.

"There's no point in it, Julia."

They'd talked about this, too. Once upon a time, his agent, Margie O'Keefe, had negotiated some pretty good deals for him, minor roles in bigger studio productions that had been "near misses" at the box office, a couple of recurrent appearances in daytime soap operas. But over the years, his marketability had waned, and Margie had plenty of younger clients to occupy her time and attention. If she dropped him now, he knew he'd never find another to take her place.

"Look," he said with a sigh. "I'm sure this whole corona virus thing is going to blow over in no time. I bet any day now, Horn comes back to let us know we've got the green light again."

In the background of the line, he heard Lucy's high-pitched voice. Julia turned her attention from the phone momentarily. "Alright, honey, yes, give me a second," she said, then glanced back at Paul. "She has a loose tooth," she said, adding drily, "Here's hoping the Tooth Fairy doesn't need to come and visit before your next big starring role."

"Yeah, ha, ha," he said as she passed the phone back to their daughter.

"Daddy!" Lucy cried. "My tooth is loose!"

"So I heard."

"You want to see?" Without waiting for a reply, she opened her mouth wide and used her fingertip to wiggle one pearly little nub on the bottom. "See?" she asked, only with her finger in her mouth, it came out: *Thee?*

"Wow, cool." Paul couldn't help but smile. He and Julia hadn't done a lot of things well in their relationship, and hell, plenty of things they'd gotten dead-ass *wrong*, but Lucy wasn't one of them. In fact, she was the only thing in his whole entire life—never mind his marriage—that he'd actually done *right*.

"Did you get it good and clean when you brushed?" he asked, and when she nodded, he pretended to frown. "You sure?"

She nodded, all round and ingenuous eyes. "I'm sure, Daddy. Did you get your teeth good and clean?"

"I haven't even brushed them yet," he admitted with a chuckle. "I guess that makes you the winner of…"

His voice faded as he looked down. Only moments earlier, he'd taken his toothbrush out and set it down on the side of the sink. Or at least, he thought he had, because now there was no sign of it on the counter.

What the…? he thought as, puzzled, he took a step back from the vanity and looked on the floor. No toothbrush. Had he knocked it accidentally into the trash can? He sifted vainly through the scant contents.

That's weird, he thought, because he could've sworn he'd just had the damn thing.

"You okay, Daddy?" Lucy asked, drawing his attention back to the phone.

"Yeah, punkin. You…uh…go on and get to bed, okay? Have you picked out a book yet for Mommy to read to you?"

She nodded. *"Fox in Socks."*

Julia hated Dr. Seuss books in general, and *Fox in Socks* in particular, because the fast-paced rhymes were basically exercises in verbal torture disguised as charming children's bedtime fare.

"I'm sure Mommy can't wait," he told Lucy, then blew her a kiss. "Night-night, punkin. I love you."

When the call ended, he crouched down to look under the sink again for his toothbrush. No luck. He dug through his toiletries bag, then moved things around on the countertop, looking beneath the hand towel and behind the display of sample-sized shampoo and conditioner the maid had left out after cleaning his room.

"What the hell?" he said, because toothbrushes didn't just sprout legs and walk away. And he'd just *seen* it, had held it *in his hand,* for Christ's sake.

Hadn't he?

"Fuck it," he muttered, deciding to just go down to the lobby and buy another.

And with my luck, I'll go all the way down there, get one, then find mine as soon as I come back to the —

The thought withered as he stepped out of the bathroom and saw his toothbrush lying on the bed, atop the crisp, white duvet.

What the hell?

Paul looked around. His room was a suite, with the bedroom adjoining a small living room area. He crossed from the former into the latter now, checking to see if anyone was there, someone from the cast or crew trying to punk him. He and the cinematographer, Terry, had worked on a few pictures together in the past and had swapped stories a time or two over beers, but Paul didn't think of him as a friend or anything. In fact, Paul didn't think of *anyone* on the production as more than just casual acquaintances at best, which meant he was at a complete and absolute loss as to who might want to fuck with him by moving his toothbrush when he wasn't paying attention. Never mind *why.*

So I must've done it myself, he thought. *By accident if nothing else. I pulled it out of my bag while I was talking with*

Lucy, then when Julia got on the phone, I must have gotten distracted. I was annoyed with her, not paying attention, and I...

What? he couldn't help but wonder. *Threw the toothbrush over my shoulder, into the other room without realizing it, only to have it land damn-near dead center on the bed?*

He picked up the toothbrush. There had to be a logical explanation, he told himself. And after a moment, one occurred to him.

Maybe after I brushed my teeth this morning, I got distracted. So maybe I brought it in here, left it on the nightstand or something, and when the maid tidied up, she put it there to make sure I saw it. I was confused earlier on the phone with Lucy. I thought I pulled it out of my bag, but I was wrong.

That made sense. Sort of.

With a shrug, he went back into the bathroom and tucked the toothbrush inside his toiletry bag. For good measure, he zipped it closed.

◆

The alarm on his phone went off at five-thirty the following morning and, from beneath a burrow of blankets and pillows, Paul reached out blindly, smacking at it to silence it. He lingered in the darkness for another long moment, his brain caught in the fogbank between asleep and awake, then pushed the covers aside, swung his legs around, and sat up on the side of the bed.

He tried to go for a run every morning. This wasn't because he enjoyed the exercise, but rather because it was a painful necessity. He already had the fact that he was over 40 working against him when auditioning for roles. He didn't need the added complication of getting flabby. As his agent, Margie, told him: "No one wants to cast a middle-aged fat ass."

When his roles took him away from L.A., he hit the workout room in whichever hotel served as his home away from home, but with all of the corona virus crap, the Piedmont had restricted access to public areas like that. Paul didn't mind, though. The woods surrounding the hotel stretched out in all directions, following the contours of the undulating landscape, and although afternoons were unseasonably hot, mornings remained crisp and cool, perfect for running outside.

That was first on his agenda, at least, after he took a piss. Barefoot, hair askew, and scratching his ass, he shuffled toward the bathroom. When he pushed the door open, he blinked in bewildered surprise to find his toiletries bag sitting open, and everything that had been inside now scattered on the counter by the sink.

Or rather, *stacked*. His hairbrush, comb, toothbrush, dental floss, razor, and deodorant—all had been somehow positioned one atop the other, with each item balanced so precisely, the makeshift tower hadn't as much as bobbled in the breeze generated when he'd opened the bathroom door.

What the hell?

He approached cautiously, examining the display from different sides and angles. He'd never seen anything like it in his life. There would be no dismissing it as something done inadvertently or blaming it on the maid. This was deliberate. Someone had built it, then left it there for him to find.

Someone…or something.

The notion of this, unexpected, made him snort out a laugh.

Yeah, right. A fucking unicorn with rainbows shooting out of its ass flew through the window in the middle of the night and did it — without fingers or opposable thumbs to boot.

Using the camera on his phone, he took several shots of the bizarre arrangement. By now, his initial surprise had given way to an almost childlike sense of fascination, and he tapped his phone, sending the pictures by text to his wife.

Look what I found in my bathroom this morning, he wrote. *Have NO clue how it got there.*

Julia was in another time zone; it was still the middle of the night there, but he felt excited and didn't have anyone else with whom he could share. He tried not to dwell on how pathetic that realization sounded.

Paul left the bathroom and went into the living room. He doublechecked the locks on his room door, and found them all secure and in place, just as he'd left them the night before. He opened the door and leaned out into the hallway, glancing first in one direction, then the next. From the looks of things, no one had surreptitiously entered his room overnight — unicorn, maid, or otherwise. How in the hell, then, could he explain what had happened in the bathroom?

I can't, he thought, and that realization niggled at him.

Returning to the bathroom, he again studied the tower. He reached out to touch the deodorant, hesitated momentarily, then gave it a light prod. At this, the entire structure came crashing down, tumbling noisily to the floor. Paul jumped back in start, then swore under his breath.

"Goddamn it." Kneeling down, he began collecting his things, shoving them back into the toiletries pouch. *Sorry, Unicorn,* he thought. *Or whoever the hell did this. Didn't mean to trash all your hard work.*

Outside the hotel, Paul weaved his way around the veritable horde of feral cats that congregated along the front steps and portico. When he'd first arrived, one of the hotel employees had explained the cats helped keep the mice population down, and were relatively harmless, but Paul, who was a dog person, found them to be a collective pain in the ass.

"Get lost," he muttered, using his foot to nudge a grey-and-black striped tabby out of his way. The cat cut him a dark look and a hiss of protest, then slinked beneath the nearest boxwood shrub.

He went for his run, the sharp mountain air clearing his mind and senses. By the time he returned to the Piedmont, patches of sweat dampened his T-shirt beneath his arms and down his back, and he felt ready to put the weird beginning to his day behind him. It was early enough yet for the lobby to still be relatively empty and quiet, and as he waited for an elevator to reach the ground floor, he had a few moments to look at some of the vintage photographs from the Piedmont's past framed on the nearby walls.

Several showed exterior views of the hotel in different seasons and time periods, most in faded black-and-white or sepia tones. One in particular caught his eye, a portrait of the

Piedmont's entrance. A crowd of people had gathered on the front steps in clothing styles he estimated to be from the early 1900s: women with broad-brimmed hats and long skirts; men in top hats and waistcoats; little girls with oversized bows in their hair and boys in sailor suits. *March 30, 1902* had been inscribed by hand in the bottom corner, with *Easter Sunday* written directly beneath.

He probably wouldn't have given it anymore thought had he not discovered the exact same picture hanging in the living room of his suite. He hadn't paid it any mind since he'd first checked in, but noticed it now immediately upon his return. At first, he thought surely it couldn't be the same print, but upon closer inspection and seeing *March 30, 1902, Easter Sunday* in the corner, he realized it was.

That's weird, he thought, although it made a certain sense, he supposed. If the hotel was that damn old, using pictures of it as the principal décor pieces seemed fitting.

Tossing his key card down on a table, he walked into the bedroom, pausing long enough to peek into the bathroom. Everything remained as it had been when he'd left, no more peculiar sculptures fashioned out of his belongings.

Which suited Paul just fine.

With film production on hold, craft services were no longer available, which meant no more free food. The hotel's restaurant had been temporarily closed because of the quarantine, so he placed a call to room service and ordered the cheapest breakfast he could: a bowl of plain oatmeal for $15. He'd had this every morning since production had stopped, because the next least-expensive alternative, a spinach omelet, clocked in ridiculously at $24. In retrospect, he was glad to have found his toothbrush, however it had happened. *Otherwise, I'd probably have to sell a kidney or something to pay for a new one from here.*

It wasn't long before he heard a knock, signaling the arrival of his food. Pulling on one of the paper masks the hotel had provided to cover his mouth and nose, he answered the door.

"Good morning, sir," said the kid who'd delivered it. He wore a mask of his own and a name tag that read *Carlos*. "I've brought your breakfast."

He lifted the dome-shaped lid covering a tray on the rolling cart in front of him, revealing the inglorious bowl of oatmeal. It looked ridiculously out of place, especially framed by a linen napkin and elaborate set of flatware, like Paul had ordered the filet mignon dinner instead.

"Great." He tried to muster some feigned enthusiasm as he stepped aside, allowing Carlos to wheel the cart into the living room. He offered the kid a couple of bucks as a tip and hoped he wouldn't be insulted by the paltry amount. To his credit, Carlos accepted the bills without any qualms, tucking them into an inner pocket in his uniform jacket.

"Thank you, sir," he said. As he turned to go, Paul cleared his throat conspicuously.

"Hey, has anything ever…happened in this room, do you know?"

Carlos looked puzzled. "What do you mean?"

"The Piedmont's supposed to be haunted, right? I was just wondering if anything specific happened here? In this room?"

Carlos gave a shrug. "No, sir, not that I know of."

"Oh," Paul said.

"My mom, though," Carlos said after a thoughtful pause. "She's worked here for years in reservations. She says the Piedmont is a portal."

"A what?"

"A portal. You know, like a door."

Paul frowned. "To what?"

"The spirit world," Carlos said. "And spirits come in and out through it all the time. It's not 'this room' or 'that area' in the Piedmont that's haunted. The *entire hotel* is."

Paul chewed on this for a moment. "So, the spirits that come through the portal…are they good? Or bad?"

"Lots of living people walk in and out of the hotel every day," Carlos said. "Some good, some bad. Same goes for spirits, I guess. Anyway, that's what my mom says." He lifted his hand in a wave as he left the suite. "Have a good rest of your day."

"Yeah," Paul murmured, closing the door behind him. "You, too."

◆

"Did you see the pictures I sent to you?" he asked Julia by Facetime later in the day.

"Yeah." Julia looked less than enthused. "Neat trick. I see you're using your time during the production lag well."

"It's not a trick. I didn't do it."

"Then who did?"

"I have no idea. I found it all that way."

"You should tell the front desk," she said. "They need to know their maids are going through their guests' personal belongings."

"It wasn't a maid. This was the middle of the night."

"They have pass keys, Paul."

"It wasn't a maid," he said again.

"Then who was it?" she asked, dubious. "A ghost? Give me a break."

"What? The Piedmont's supposedly haunted."

"*Supposedly*," she repeated with pointed emphasis. "What's with you? You've never believed in stuff like that. You make fun of all those ghost-hunting shows on TV."

"I didn't say I believed it. *You* suggested a ghost, not me."

"Whatever." She rolled her eyes. He could hear Lucy again, muted in the background, asking for the phone. Which only made Julia roll her eyes again. "Your daughter wants to talk to you."

He started to say something in response but may as well have saved his breath. She'd already passed the phone to Lucy.

"Daddy!" she exclaimed.

"Lucy!" he exclaimed in reply, making her laugh. At least momentarily, then her nose wrinkled, and her expression grew solemn. "Did you see a ghost?"

"What? No. Don't be silly. There's no such thing."

"I heard Mommy say you saw a ghost."

"Well, Mommy's wrong," he said, dropping Lucy a wink. "I don't know what's gotten into her. Maybe it's rabies. We're probably going to have to call Grandma and Grandpa and have them—"

"Stop it, Daddy." Lucy had broken out in a giggle fit. "Mommy doesn't have rabies."

From somewhere in the background, he heard Julia utter an indignant squawk.

While Lucy chattered about her day so far, which consisted of watching *Paw Patrol*, *Miraculous Ladybug*, and *Wild Kratts* on TV, and having a grilled cheese sandwich with Cheeto's for lunch, he found himself distracted by the old photo of the Piedmont hanging on the living room wall. His gaze wandered again to the faded image, the guests and dignitaries who had gathered on that Easter Sunday almost 120 years ago.

This time he noticed something.

The exterior of the Piedmont looked straight out of a gothic movie, all slate-grey stone, solemn arches, and sharply peaked turrets. It stretched out in different wings that, from an aerial shot, Paul imagined would look like a groping hand, fingers outstretched. The main part of the hotel, the *corps de logis*, towered above the rest at thirteen stories high, and in the photograph from 1902, Paul could see an indistinct figure leaning out one of the windows on this topmost floor.

Not just leaning, he thought, and he went back to the bedroom to retrieve his reading glasses from the nightstand. Slipping them on, he again examined the photo. It was impossible to tell if it was a man or woman, adult or child, but one thing was horrifyingly obvious: the figure in the thirteenth floor window wasn't just leaning out—they were *falling*.

"Shit," Paul said, completely forgetting he was on the phone with his five-year-old daughter.

"Daddy," she gasped. "You said a potty word!"

"I...I'm sorry, punkin," he said, mortified. "It just slipped out. I...saw something, that's all."

"Saw what?'

"A...uh...a cat," he said, for some reason his mind turning to that cluster of feral fleabags that lived on the hotel grounds. "I...uh...have my window open and one of them jumped onto the ledge from outside."

Up thirteen stories, at that, he thought, because that's where his room was, number 1305.

"A kitty?" she exclaimed in abject delight. "Can we keep it?"

"What?" he said, imagining Julia overhearing this, her jaw hitting the floor. "No, no, we can't keep it. I chased it away. It's wild, like an alley cat. There's a bunch of them living in the woods around the hotel."

"Oh."

She pouted, clearly disappointed, and he felt a momentary pang of guilt. "I'm sorry, punkin."

"That's okay," she mumbled.

When she handed the phone off, Julia glared at him through the screen.

"I'm sorry," he said.

"Whatever, Paul."

"I'm serious. I'm sorry," he said, flipping the camera view so that he could show her the photograph. "Look what I found. This is hanging on the wall in my hotel room. It's the Piedmont, back in 1902."

"Stop trying to change the subject."

"I'm not. Look. This is freaky." He pointed to the blurry figure, then watched Julia wrinkle her nose, squinting at it. "Do you see it?"

"See what?"

"There's somebody falling out of that window."

She half-laughed. "What?"

"Look," he told her, pointing again. "Right there."

"Paul, I'm not doing this right now. Lucy just ran into her bedroom crying…"

"What?" Now he felt more than a twinge of guilt; he felt like full-fledged, steaming hot shit on a shingle.

"…and I'm going to go after her so I can try to fix the mess you made by telling her she can't have a cat."

"I didn't say that."

"No, *I'm* the one who's stuck telling her, because we can't have one with our lease." Just before the screen went dark as she disconnected the call, she added coldly, "And you know it."

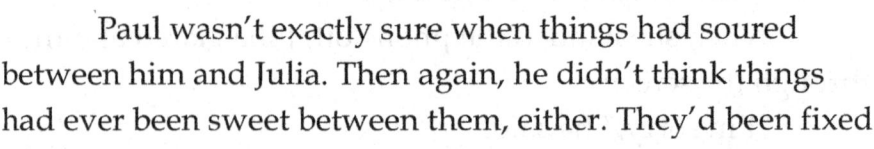

Paul wasn't exactly sure when things had soured between him and Julia. Then again, he didn't think things had ever been sweet between them, either. They'd been fixed up together by well-intentioned friends, dated for a handful of months, then decided to tie the knot after Julia found out she was pregnant. She'd quit her job to be a full-time mom, while he'd shouldered the responsibility of household provider. She made no secret of the fact that she resented the hell out of him for the sacrifices she'd made, and he made no secret that he likewise resented her for his own.

Had they ever loved each other? He couldn't say for sure, one way or the other, but they both loved Lucy. That had been enough to make things work up to now. How much longer that would be the case remained to be seen.

With a heavy sigh, he sat down on the couch, cradling his phone in his hand. He thought about calling Julia again, trying to smooth things over, not just with her but with Lucy, too. Instead, though, he tapped to open his internet browser, and in the search bar, he typed: *Piedmont Hotel, Easter 1902, accident.*

The Piedmont's website link popped up first in the results, followed by a slew of links to different online articles and resources documenting the plethora of ghost stories and spooky happenings associated with the hotel. Nothing specifically pertaining to Easter, 1902 that he could find, so he amended his search terms and tried again: *Piedmont Hotel, Easter death.*

Still no luck. There were reports of people who had died at the Piedmont over the years—apparently a metric shit-ton, Paul discovered to his surprise—but nothing he could relate directly to Easter Sunday, 1902, and the ghostly figure he saw in the photograph on the wall.

He decided to return to the hotel lobby and re-examine the copy hanging near the main elevators. Maybe it would offer a clearer image of the figure at the window, or maybe there would be other photographs from that same date on display that he could use for comparison.

The cast and crew of *Hotel Evil* occupied the entire thirteenth floor, and although the corridor was empty as he stepped out of his room, from behind thin walls and neighboring doors, he could hear a muted chorus of sounds: people talking, TVs and radios playing. The room numbers ascended the further from the elevators they were located, with the last, Room 1313, at the far end of the hall. He glanced in that direction, and felt a strange shiver go through him, the hairs along the nape of his neck stirring uneasily. Curiously, the quality of light seemed to change as it approached that last room, growing dimmer, a shroud of shadows enveloping the corridor.

Wonder whose room that is, he thought, glad it wasn't his at any rate, because he'd give himself the creeps if he had to cross through that dimly lit area to get to and from the elevator. Then something else occurred to him. The figure he'd seen in the photo in his room had been falling from a window on the distalmost side on the thirteenth floor. Which would mean…

He would have been in Room 1313.

Instantly forgetting his initial reservations, he changed course and headed away from the elevators. The closer he came to Room 1313, the more the sounds from the other rooms seemed to fall away, until a heavy, nearly palpable sort of silence engulfed him. The air felt strangely heavy all at once, thick and almost muggy, enough to leave a thin sheen of perspiration blooming across his brow. He raised his fist to knock on the door and realized his hand was shaking.

What's wrong with me? he thought, taking a moment to mop his clammy palm against the leg of his jeans. *It's just a room, for Christ's sake. Four walls and some furniture.*

And a window.

He knocked, then waited a moment, breath bated, head cocked as he strained to hear anything from inside the room. He had no idea to whom Room 1313 had been assigned. Hell, for all he knew, whoever was in there was sound asleep, taking an afternoon nap, and he was disturbing them.

When he had no response, heard no sounds after a moment, he tried again, louder this time. Still no answer. Paul glanced back in the direction of the elevators, found the hallway remained deserted, then decided what the hell and tried the door knob.

To his astonishment, it turned in his hand, the room unlocked. After another uncertain glance around him to make sure the coast was clear, he eased the door open slowly, allowing him a peek inside.

"Hello?" he called quietly.

No response. The door swung all of the way open, presenting him with an unobstructed view of the suite beyond. The layout pretty much matched his own; he found himself facing a living room, with an adjacent bedroom to the left.

"Hello?" he called again, venturing across the threshold, leaving the door ajar behind him. "Anyone home?"

He saw no signs that the room was occupied. Everything from the glossy, cherry-stained furnishings to the caramel-colored upholstery looked pristine and unblemished. In the bedroom, he could see the king-sized bed was perfectly made, the pillows artfully arranged. He could also see the bedroom window.

The one in the photograph.

Curious, he looked around, wondering if the same print from the lobby would be there somewhere, too. There were several prints framed and hanging on the walls, along with a large painting of the Piedmont, a stoic sentry against its backdrop of wooded mountains.

Paul walked into the bedroom and slowly approached the window. Parting the filmy drapes with his hands, he found himself looking down at the hotel's circular front drive and expansive yard. He tried to imagine the photo from 1902, only this time from the perspective of the person who'd been in that very spot on that Easter Sunday, the poor son of a bitch who'd gazed at the same scene, perhaps able to hear the excited voices from those gathered on the steps below. Had he leaned out too far to try and get a better look?

Turning the brass latch, Paul unlocked the window, then pushed it open. Hotel maintenance workers hadn't replaced the screen inserts with winter storm windows yet, and he could feel the press of the breeze filter in. He popped the screen out and set it on the floor nearby, propped against the wall. Bracing his hands against the window sill, he ducked his head to avoid the sash and leaned out.

The sun was bright and warm, the wind crisp and cool. He looked down at the steep pitch of the slate roof, the abrupt drop-off just past the copper gutter lining the edge. The realization of just how far he was from the ground left him feeling vaguely lightheaded and dizzy, and he retreated back inside again.

From behind him, he heard a quiet creak and spun in surprise. He caught a glimpse of movement: the bathroom door swinging open slowly. The lights were off inside, but he saw daylight from the window reflect in a flash off the mirror above the sink. And with this sharp glint of illumination, he saw something else inside the bathroom.

What the...? Leaving the window sash raised behind him, he walked briskly across the room. He pushed the bathroom door fully open, then turned on the lights, squinting against the glare. When his vision adjusted, he saw a tower of toiletries on the countertop — toothbrush, razor, deodorant, dental floss — all aligned in precarious but perfect balance.

Wait just a fucking minute... His eyes widened in new surprise. *Are those mine?*

He recognized his hairbrush by the chip out of the handle, which he'd lost when he'd accidentally dropped it several months earlier. The deodorant was his, too, a variation of Old Spice called "Wolfthorn" that he'd bought because Julia had laughed her ass off about it at the store.

"Made with real, grade-A wolf piss," she'd gravely intoned, seconds before they'd both broken down in hysterics in the middle of the personal care aisle at Walgreens. Lucy had laughed with them, even though she hadn't really understood what was so funny.

What the fuck is going on? he thought in bewildered alarm as he stood in the bathroom of Room 1313. *These are all my things! How did they get here? How the fuck did — ?*

From the direction of the living room, he heard a loud bang as the door to the suite slammed shut. Heart pounding, eyes flown wide, Paul raced out of the bathroom. He grabbed the front door by the handle and tried to twist it, but nothing happened. It spun in his hands, the way a rabbit's head will loll on the stalk of its neck once you've stomped it hard enough with your boot. He couldn't get it to catch, couldn't get the door open, and after a moment of impotent, futile trying, he uttered a hoarse, panicked cry.

"Hey!" Balling his fist, he pounded on the door. "Hey, let me out! Open the door!"

He heard a peculiar sound from somewhere off to his left, like something heavy being dragged across the dense nap of the carpeting. He glanced in that direction, then recoiled in surprise to find a large armoire that had been flush against the far wall now in the middle of the room. Not only that, but the chair that had been in one of the corners had somehow moved toward the center, too, and the couch seemed to have pivoted a good 30 degrees, as if it had been turned to better face the door to the suite — and Paul.

"What the fuck?" he whispered.

Another groaning creak, and a table to his right, just past the entry, suddenly moved, first one half of it swinging around, then the other, as if somehow — impossibly — alive and shambling toward him.

"Jesus!"

The oversized painting of the Piedmont that hung above the table abruptly flew from the wall as if launched by a catapult. With a cry, Paul floundered back, lost his footing, and fell onto his ass just as it careened over his head, smashing into a nearby wall. Before his stunned mind could fully process the fact that he could have easily just been decapitated by the goddamn thing, he heard that awful, ominous scraping again and saw the armoire scoot itself forward, much as the table had done.

This isn't real, he thought, stumbling to his feet. *Furniture doesn't move. Not by itself. This can't be happening.*

But even as he tried to convince himself, the table lumbered like some disjointed, oversized spider to block his access to the door. The chair slewed across the carpet to position itself close by, as if offering backup to the table. One end of the couch swung in a wide arc, sweeping toward him, forcing him to scramble out of the way, back toward the bedroom.

"This isn't real," he said, groping for his pocket, yanking out his phone. Before he could unlock the screen, never mind call for help, the cord from a nearby lamp whipped loose from the wall outlet, lashing out and coiling around his wrist. It snapped painfully taut, then wrenched his arm, forcing him to drop the phone.

"Let go of me," he cried, tearing at the cord with his free hand, struggling to wedge his fingertips beneath it. He could feel it clamping off his circulation, could see the sudden, terrifying purple-red flush of his hand.

"Get off me!" he shrieked, abandoning his attempt to free himself, and instead, jerking on the length of cord itself, dragging the lamp within reach. Curling his fingers around the brass base, he began smashing it into the nearest wall over and over, crumpling the shade, splintering the shaft. "Get off me! Get off, get off, *get the fuck off me!*"

As he lurched blindly backwards, waltzing with the lamp and cord, he felt something soft and yielding underfoot. He glanced down, saw he'd stepped on a corner of the bedsheet that had somehow wound up splayed across the floor—then it leaped from the floor like a snake striking. In an instant, it wound its way up the length of his leg, from ankle to thigh, enveloping him like mummy wrappings. He screamed again, floundering across the bedroom, tangled up and struggling.

"*Help!* Somebody help me!"

With a snap of splintering wood and a screech of metal springs contorting, the entire bed began to move, the headboard rising and twisting as if to look at him, while the footboard scrabbled toward him, one corner at a time. The phone receiver lifted away from the base, bobbing on its cord as it floated in mid-air like a cobra. More furniture slid around to flank him in a tight circumference

What's happening? Paul thought wildly, still grasping the broken lamp in one hand as he stumbled backwards. *Oh,*

God, what the fuck is happening? This can't be real. This isn't possible. It's not—

He felt his ass hit the edge of the window sill. At that exact moment, the sheet around his leg abruptly constricted and he shrieked in sudden agony as the 1,000-thread-count Egyptian cotton somehow compressed hard and fast enough to shatter the bones in his leg from his hip down. When the sheet then whipped away from him, unfurling as quickly as if withdrawn on a winch, the momentum sent Paul careening off-balance in an agonizing, clumsy semi-circle.

As he started to fall toward the window and the steep plummet just beyond, he found himself faced with his own ghostly reflection against the window glass—ashen, wide-eyed, and open-mouthed, a better masque of horror than anything he could have ever affected on-camera.

He wasn't now, nor had he ever been, that great an actor.

The Stranger

I've grown so accustomed to John's absence, when I first wake up and feel nothing next to me but cool, empty space on his side of the bed, I don't feel puzzled or alarmed. As my mind makes the slow shift from unconsciousness to awake, however, it occurs to me dimly: *John's home now, back on Earth.*

I open my eyes and see moonlight filtering through the window. The blankets lay turned back where he pushed them aside, and a fading indentation remains from where his head had rested against the pillow.

"John?" I squint in the direction of the bathroom. The door is ajar, the lights off, the room clearly vacant.

He looked thin to me when I first saw him upon his return, haggard and gaunt, even though I expected this. The other astronauts' wives had forewarned me.

"It's the weightlessness," Denise had tried to explain. "Six months or more with no gravity, and your muscles start to shrink, no matter how much you exercise."

Even so, his appearance had shocked me, and I'd tried not to cry, because it would upset him. And besides, I'd told myself at the time, the most important thing was that he was home again, safe and sound, and not every other astronaut's wife was lucky enough to say as much.

Like Susan Manning.

Susan's husband Dave had been part of John's crew. On the fourth month aboard the Nomad, Dave went on a spacewalk to install additional bracket supports for the station's solar arrays. Something had gone wrong; Dave's suit integrity had been compromised and started to depressurize. Why he hadn't returned to the space station remains a mystery.

If Dave had realized what was happening in time, at least enough to huff out his breath and empty his lungs, he might have suffered little more than some frostbite, and perhaps lost consciousness, at least until one of his crewmates had been able to haul him back aboard the Nomad. But Dave either hadn't realized, or he'd panicked whenever he did, because instead of breathing out to avoid one hell of a case of the bends, he'd apparently sucked in a deep, whooping gasp, as evidenced by the fact his lungs had ruptured, collapsing like wadded scraps of old newsprint bound for the trash. By the time anyone had been able to reach him, it was too late.

"John?" I call again, taking my robe from the end of the bed.

The funeral would be tomorrow at noon, and in the meantime, I've tried everything I can to take John's mind — and my own — off of the terrible tragedy. To celebrate his homecoming, I made his favorite dinner: a London broil, roasted new potatoes, and creamed spinach. But although he'd smiled politely at it all and offered mumbled praise about how delicious everything looked, he'd hardly done more than poke at it with his fork.

"John?" When I reach the base of the staircase, I feel a sudden breeze and find the patio door open. The yard beyond lies shadow-draped and dark, with only the waning moon overhead casting a spill of pale illumination across the grass. Bathed in this eerie glow, John stands with his head tipped back as he looks up at the sky.

"John," I say, hurrying toward him. "What are you doing?"

I touch his shoulder, and he startles, whirling to look at me. For a moment, it's like being regarded by a stranger—as if he's never laid eyes on me before in his life.

"What are you doing out here?" I ask again.

"I don't know." His voice falters. "I couldn't sleep."

I take him by the hand. "Come on. Let's go back inside."

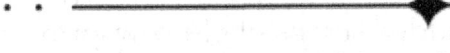

The next day, NASA sends a car to take us to the funeral, and when it arrives, the driver honks the horn to alert us.

"John?" I call as I slide the back onto a pearl stud in my left ear. "The car's here."

He doesn't answer and I hurry up to the second floor. I find him in the master bathroom, facing his reflection in the mirror.

"Honey," I say, trying not to sound aggravated, reminding myself that I'm glad he's home, and that it could just as well be his wake I was getting ready to attend as Dave Manning's. "The car just pulled up. Are you ready?"

He meets my gaze through the mirror. His expression is flat, unreadable. "Yes," he says. "Let's go."

As we approach, I see news vans parked near the statehouse where the memorial service is being held. Although interest in space flights has withered over the years, an astronaut dying still piques enough media interest to warrant coverage. Every flag along the exterior grounds has been lowered to half-staff in Dave's honor, and limousines delivering state officials and members of Congress line the street.

Our driver drops us off at the base of the broad staircase leading up to the main portico, and I hook my hand against John's elbow as we make our way toward the top. As we walk, I shoot glances at him, trying to gauge how he's doing, but he keeps his mouth set in a thin line, his face a mask of stoic impassivity.

Inside the rotunda, I see poor Susan Manning standing at the head of a lengthy receiving line. There's no casket, only a large, framed portrait on a tripod. In the photograph, Dave smiles confidently at the camera, clad in an orange space suit, his helmet against his hip.

Two men flank Susan on either side: one in a military dress uniform I recognize as Colonel Arthur Graham, operations director for the Nomad Program, and Robert Kingsley, mission control flight director. Susan stands somewhat behind them as mourners approach in slow-moving procession, and God, she looks awful: as pale and gaunt as a corpse herself, with shadow-rimmed and sunken eyes, her glassy gaze seemingly focused on a point beyond the gathered crowd, or rather through us, as if we're all made of glass. They must have given her something. A Valium, maybe. Or an entire fifth of vodka.

"John," Colonel Graham says when it's our turn to approach. "Mary, how good of you both to come."

"Thank you, sir," John says, accepting his proffered hand clasp. He draws in a breath to say more, maybe greet Robert Kingsley, then Susan speaks — the first words I've heard her utter to anyone.

"John?" The shellshocked glaze in her eyes lifts somewhat, and she looks like a lost child, alone in the woods in the dead of the night. Although both Kingsley and Graham try to stop her with murmurs of protest, she pushes past them. "John!"

John stiffens, looking stricken and I wade clumsily to his rescue. "We're so terribly sorry, Susan," I say, words that sound empty and meaningless. "So heartbroken for you."

Susan ignores my pitiful attempt at condolences, looking up at John with round, pleading eyes. "What happened?"

It's a peculiar question because she must know. They'd told me and Denise, the other crew-members' wives. Susan had to know.

"They won't let me see him," Susan says to John. "What happened out there? I know you know the truth."

Her voice scrapes like fingernails shorn to the nubs against the slate of a chalkboard, and Graham and Kingsley both catch her gently by the shoulders. At this, as if summoning some inner reserve of strength, Susan utters a hoarse cry and shrugs herself free from them, all but lunging at John again.

"They won't let me see him," she cries, and begins to pummel him with her fists, striking at his shoulders, neck, and face. "You were there. I know you know. Tell me what happened to Dave! Tell me the truth, goddamn you!"

Wearing sheepish expressions of apology, Kingsley and Graham wrestle her away. She struggles again but only briefly, feebly this time, then bursts into tears, clapping her hands over her face.

"They won't…let me see him…" she sobs. Kingsley steers her in a stumbling semi-circle, then ushers her away toward the far side of the rotunda and a doorway marked with an exit sign.

"I'm so sorry," Colonel Graham says. "Are you alright, John?"

"Y-yes," John says, but his shirt is rumpled, his tie askew, and I can see a red splotch blooming on one of his cheeks where she'd struck him.

"She isn't well," Graham continues. "Of course, it's understandable given the circumstances."

"Of…course," John says, and besides that scarlet point of impact on the arch of his cheek, his face is pale, nearly ashen in hue, as if he might vomit.

"Why don't you step out for a few moments? Get some fresh air." Graham must notice his sudden pallor, too. "Use the side doors. The press can't get past security there to follow you."

◆

"Are you alright?" someone asks.

I'm leaning over one of the sinks in the ladies' room, dabbing at my face with a damp paper towel and trying to avoid smudging my mascara in the process. Lifting my head, I see her through the mirror, a woman with dark hair who looks vaguely familiar.

"I...I'm fine," I say with a weak smile. "Thank you."

I hope this reassurance is enough to make her go away, because I really don't feel like talking to anyone right now.

"Are you sure?" the woman asks, and her expression shifts as, almost apologetically, she adds, "I saw what happened in the rotunda."

"I'm fine," I say again, but my hand is shaking as I reach for another paper towel.

She beats me to it, then offers one to me. "Poor Susan."

"I know," I say, with an added murmur of thanks. As I pat my cheek dry, I try to figure out where I know this woman from, where I've seen her before. Maybe a holiday party for mission control or the crew.

"Have they told you anything about what happened?" she asks.

"To Dave?" I say and she nods. "Just that his suit integrity failed."

"Your husband hasn't said anything otherwise?"

Tell me the truth, goddamn you! Susan's words echo briefly in my mind. I find my smile growing harder to hold.

"You make it sound like there's something more to tell," I say, sidestepping to move around her, make my way toward the door. I don't know who this woman is, but the way she asked that, the way she turns her back to the mirror now and leans against the edge of the sink, makes me feel decidedly uneasy.

Folding her arms across her chest, she says, "Something hit the station."

I blink at her, caught off guard. "What?"

"Something hit the station," she says again.

"You mean when Dave was killed? During the spacewalk?"

She studies me for a moment. "I'm not even sure there really was a spacewalk."

"Of...of course, there was," I say with a bark of bewildered laughter. "There were dozens of them during the mission. And probably lots of things that hit the station, too. The upper atmosphere is full of space debris."

This floating flotsam and jetsam was left over from long-dead satellites, rocket parts from long-ago missions, and other junk trapped in endless orbit. The Nomad had been hit by it before, plenty of times, and suffered close calls even more frequently than that. More often than not, it was no big deal, and when collisions with larger objects were deemed imminent, the station would be temporarily evacuated, the crew dispatched to the capsules until the danger had passed. And they sure as hell wouldn't have allowed anyone outside.

"Not debris," the woman tells me. "Something from outside the atmosphere. From space, big enough to knock out the Nomad's satellite arrays and cause a communication blackout onboard. They don't know the full extent of the damage, because a lot of the computer systems are still down."

She turns around and leans toward the mirror, drawing her upper lip back as if checking for lipstick residue on her teeth. "Then there's what happened to the Russians."

"I...I'm sorry. What did you say your name was?"

"It's Gretchen." She turns to offer her hand. "Gretchen Nettles."

Too late, I realize where I've seen her before—not at any NASA potluck, but on my television screen.

"You're a reporter." I leave her hand unshaken, hanging in the open air.

"A correspondent," she says as if correcting me, as if there's a difference, a distinction somehow in the semantics.

"We were told this area's off limits to the press. How did you get in?"

"Mrs. Dupain, don't you want to know? What happened to Dave Manning, it could have easily been your husband."

"I don't know what you're talking about." I shove past her and hurry out the bathroom door. "Excuse me."

◆

I find John outside on an otherwise vacant portico overlooking the statehouse grounds, cradling a cigarette in his hand. "I'd like to go," he tells me, taking one last, sharp drag before flicking the still-smoldering butt beyond the balustrade. "Do you mind?"

I shake my head. "Of course not."

I don't tell him what happened in the ladies' room. But as we sit together in the back seat on the car ride home, I can't help but think about what Gretchen Nettles had said. And what she'd left unsaid.

Then there's what happened to the Russians. What did that mean? I feel stupid now for not asking about it at the time, but the whole encounter had caught me off guard, especially in light of what happened with Susan in the rotunda.

Different countries had helped to fund and develop the Nomad program and collectively shared the space station. During John's mission, there had been three crewmembers from Russia aboard, along with three from the United States.

Something hit the ship…something from outside the atmosphere. From space.

If this was true, had it damaged more than the Nomad's satellite arrays? Had the Russian crewmembers been injured as a result?

Or worse?

I don't want to ask John, at least not right now. He sits rigidly in his seat, as if at attention, his gaze fixed beyond the smoky glass of the tinted window. He reaches up almost absently to rub at his eye…no, not rub, but rather to press his fingertips lightly beneath it, treacherously close to the edge of his lower lid, as if feeling for something there.

When we get home, he walks wordlessly into his office and closes the door behind him, an unveiled hint that he didn't want to be disturbed.

◆

Two days pass, and Denise invites me over for coffee. We sit together in the kitchen while the percolator gurgles, and she slices us each thick wedges from a lemon-flavored bundt cake she tells me she made from scratch, a recipe she found in *Good Housekeeping.*

"I don't know why I even bother," she laments. With the flap of a hand, she indicates beyond the sliding glass doors toward the patio and a large in-ground swimming pool in which her sons, nine-year-old identical twins, splash and play. "The boys won't eat anything that doesn't come out of a can or with its own powdered cheese packet included. And Guy can't have sweets, says he has to keep his weight down, even between missions. Still, the house smells so good when there's something baking."

Like everything Denise makes, the lemon cake is heavy-handed on sugar, so cloying and sweet, one bite makes my teeth hurt.

"So, tell me." She reaches for her cigarette pack and slips one between her lips, leaving an ever-so-slight smutch of lipstick on the filter. "What happened at the wake?" With a snap of her lighter, the cigarette is ablaze, and she tips her head back, blowing out a quick stream of smoke. "I heard Susan caused quite the scene when you and John arrived."

"It wasn't a scene really." A part of me longs to tell Denise about what had happened after that, Gretchen following me into the restroom, but I know she's a gossiping sort. "I think she just broke down."

"Poor thing," Denise says, her elbow propped on the table, cigarette cocked in her hand. "They took her to Western State Hospital after that, you know." When I blink in surprise, she nods. "An involuntary hold."

"For how long?" I ask, horrified.

"Who can say?" Denise replies with a shrug. "I've heard only seventy-two hours, but with a court order, they can go much longer. Weeks, even months at a time."

From outside, the boys shriek as they leap wildly from the edge of the pool into the water, resulting in a violent splash that douses the concrete patio. Denise looks suddenly wistful, as if she feels envious of Susan sequestered away and doped up on benzodiazepines and phenobarbital.

The coffee is done now, so she sets her cigarette down to rest in a notch of the ashtray, pushes her chair back, and goes into the kitchen. "Maybe we could visit her," she muses. "Will they let you have visitors at a mental hospital? Surely so. I'll make cake for her. There's an icebox-chocolate recipe I've been dying to give a go…"

She continues to chatter as she opens first one cupboard, then another, pulling down teacups and saucers. I find my gaze wandering toward the nearby living room, and the framed photographs on the wall of Denise, Guy, and the twins, all bright eyes and happy smiles as they pose for family portraits.

"Has Guy seemed okay to you since he came home?" I ask and if she finds the question odd, she doesn't let on.

"I suppose. I mean, he's been sleeping a lot, but I'm used to that. He's still in bed now, in fact."

Perfectly poised so as not to slosh, she carries two cups of coffee, each atop its own saucer, back to the table, setting one in front of me, the other beside her ashtray. She plucks her cigarette up again but before returning to her chair, she goes to the sliding glass door and draws it open enough to lean outside.

"Your father is trying to sleep," she screeches at the twins. "Keep it down! If I have to warn you again, you're both inside this house until school starts back!"

With this, she slams the door shut with enough force to rattle the entire frame. Turning back to me with a strained smile, she says, "Would you like any cream for that, Mary?"

"Oh, no," I reply with an obliging sip of my coffee. "Just black is fine. Thank you."

A short time later, I excuse myself to use the restroom. The hallway from Denise's dining room seems unusually dark, the overhead light out, then I remember she told me that Guy is still sleeping in the master bedroom at the far end. The bathroom is directly across, and I creep quietly along, not wanting to disturb him. As I draw closer, however, I realize the door to the master bedroom on my left is ajar, and Guy is standing in the bathroom to my right. Dressed in pajama bottoms and a T-shirt, he faces the sink and takes no notice of me.

His attention is on the mirror in front of him, and he leans toward it, his hands raised to his face. With one, he pries his bottom eyelid down. With the other, he appears to be pulling something out of his eye. It's long, slender, and elastic, like a thread of taffy, only instead of pink or yellow, it's as black as pitch. It glistens under the lights like wet oil or tar, and whatever it is, it must be stuck to his eye somehow, because as he pulls, his eyeball protrudes from the socket like at any moment, with a resounding *POP!* like a bubble bursting, it would break free. I can see the smooth white orbit, threaded with red capillaries, and that dark, viscous substance protruding from the center of his iris, the dark rim of his pupil.

I must make a sound even though I'm not aware, my mind too frozen with horrified confusion at what I'm witnessing. Perhaps the floorboards squeak underfoot, or I utter a low gasp, but all at once, Guy turns to look at me. As he does, he lets go of that strange filament, and it retracts in an instant back into his eye, recoiling like the length of a tape measure with a moist, audible squelch. By the time he's facing fully in my direction, it's gone, and his eye looks normal as he regards me, his affect flat and emotionless.

"I...I'm sorry," I say.

He doesn't answer. I'm reminded of that moment when I discovered John outside in the yard in the middle of the night, when he'd looked at me as if he'd never seen me before. Guy regards me with that same curious detachment, and the only thing I can think to do is back away from him, stumbling toward the dining room again.

"Take some of this home, would you?" Denise asks as I emerge from the shadows of the hall back into the swath of sunshine spilling through the patio doors. She's already wrapped up all the remaining bundt cake with foil and sets it down on the kitchen table beside my now-cold coffee.

"You don't want it?" I ask, my voice coming out shaky and shrill.

"I told you. Nobody will eat it but me. And I already have to squeeze myself into three sets of Spanx before I look presentable in public. A moment on the lips, an eternity on the hips, that's what my mother always used to say."

I glance down the hallway and see Guy standing at the far end, cloaked in shadows, motionless and facing me.

"Of course," I gush, seizing the cake with both hands. "Well, I really should be going now."

"So soon?" Denise asks with a put-upon pout.

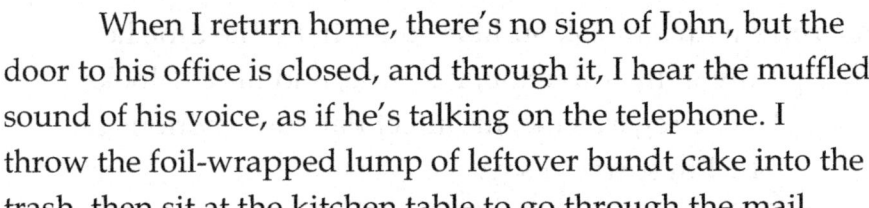

When I return home, there's no sign of John, but the door to his office is closed, and through it, I hear the muffled sound of his voice, as if he's talking on the telephone. I throw the foil-wrapped lump of leftover bundt cake into the trash, then sit at the kitchen table to go through the mail.

Surely I had been imagining things. This is what I've told myself since leaving Denise's house. That strange substance coming out of Guy's eyeball, it had all been in my head, a trick of the lights. The sooner I put it out of my mind, the better, I've decided.

As I sort past sales circulars and miscellaneous bills, a plain envelope attracts my gaze. It's addressed by hand to *MRS. JOHN DUPAIN*, and curiously, the return address lists no sender by name, only a P.O. box in Atlanta, which strikes me as strange because I don't know anyone from there.

I open it and find a handwritten note inside. It's from Gretchen Nettles, the news reporter, but even though my first instinct is to throw it away unread, the first line stops me cold:

The Russians are dead.

I glance toward the hallway, back toward John's office. Even though I can still hear the quiet murmur of his voice as he continues speaking on the phone, I can't help but feel guilty, as if this is wrong and whatever is in the letter is supposed to be a secret. But my curiosity is piqued, just like when I'd been a teenager at a slumber party, and we started a game of Would-You-Rather, so I continue to read.

Their Soyuz capsule deployed at the same time the NASA one did, Gretchen wrote. *It touched down in Kazakhstan like it was programmed to do. All of its systems checked out. But all three of the cosmonauts inside were burned to death, their bodies charred beyond recognition. The Russian government had to use dental records to identify them. There's evidence to suggest the fire started inside the capsule at some point during its descent, and that it was deliberately set by one or more of the cosmonauts.*

What she was telling me didn't make sense. Why on earth would the Russians have done something so horrible — and horrific — on purpose?

I'm sure you know this, but during re-entry, the heat that builds up outside the capsule prevents radio transmissions to Earth. But just before the Soyuz from the Nomad station entered this blackout zone, the Russian State Corporation for Space Activities received one final transmission from flight engineer Alexei Sokolov. Roughly translated, he said "it is here with us. It is in here." What he meant by this remains unknown.

From the direction of John's office, I hear the sudden, startling crash of broken glass. The letter flutters from my hand, skating off the edge of the table and falling to the floor.

"John?"

I walk down the hall but hesitate outside his door. I can no longer hear any voices from inside, only a strange and heavy silence. Again, I think of Guy standing in front of his bathroom mirror, and the way his eyeball seemed about to bulge right out of its socket as he pulled that strange, fibrous strand loose from the center.

It is here with us. It is in here.

I think of how John had been rubbing at his eye in the car on our way home from Dave Manning's funeral.

Don't be a goose, I tell myself firmly. *I'm lucky to have my husband home again, safe and sound.*

"Honey?" I rap lightly on the door. My voice sounds strained and shaky. "Are you alright?"

There is only more of that silence in response at first, then his voice through the wood, so clear it sounds like he's standing right on the other side of the door: "I'm fine."

I step back, feeling not just surprised by the proximity of his reply, but unnerved by it. "I...I thought I heard something break..."

Even though it's midday, it's dark enough in the hallway for me to see the narrow slit of light escaping from beneath the office door and the two patches of shadow interrupting it: his feet on the opposite side. I hadn't heard any movement from inside the office before I knocked and can't help but imagine now that John has been standing there at the door all that while, waiting for me.

"My cup fell," he says. "I spilled my coffee. Would you bring me some paper towels?"

"Oh," I say. "Of...of course."

I hurry back into the kitchen, pausing as I glance at the table. The letter Gretchen Nettles had sent is still on the floor. It occurs to me that John will be angry if he finds it, and I pick it up, then stuff it down in the trashcan, past Denise's lemon cake. Grabbing the paper towel roll, I return to the hallway. It seems darker than ever now, as if the shadows are heavier, closing in from all sides.

"I have them," I say and from inside the office, I hear the doorknob rattle, the click of the latch. The door swings open and John stands there, regarding me, stone-faced.

"Good," he says and as he steps aside in unspoken invitation, I think I see a glint of light across the surface of his left pupil as if something there, buried deep within that dark disk, abruptly moves.

Don't be a goose, I think again, sharper this time. It's John, for God's sake. Whatever happened to the Russians or Dave Manning doesn't matter. He's home again, safe and sound, and I'm grateful, I tell myself as I walk into the office, and he closes the door behind me.

Not every other astronaut's wife is lucky enough to say as much.

The Baxter Family's Quantum Vacation

"What the actual fuck...?"

Barbara startled awake at the sound of her daughter's voice—or more specifically, the fact that her eight year old had just cursed out loud. *Very* loudly, in fact.

"Tammy," she groaned, squinting hard as she opened her eyes and found herself looking up at a bright blue sky. *Too damn bright,* she thought, and it occurred to her that it was odd she'd heard her husband's voice just as she'd said their daughter's name, Calvin calling to Tammy.

"Watch your mouth," she heard Calvin say, which was really strange because she'd said those exact same words, at the exact same time, or at least, she *thought* she had. She'd meant to, anyway, but didn't hear her own voice, only Calvin's, offering the groggy-sounding admonition.

"You should leave him," her friend Sheila had told her two weeks earlier, as they'd sat across from each other in a small luncheonette booth, both nursing cups of lukewarm coffee.

"I know," Barbara had replied, shoulders sagging in unhappy resignation.

"He cheated on you," Sheila told her pointedly.

"I know."

"You could do so much better."

And Barbara had known that, too.

"This can't be happening," she heard Tammy say from somewhere close by. "Somebody pinch me. I mean it. Somebody fucking pinch me, and I mean right goddamn now!"

"Tammy Annmarie Barker…" Barbara heard Calvin growl in warning, and goddamn it, how was he doing that? It was like he was reading her mind, stealing her words, saying what she meant to say just as she intended to say it, and however it was happening, she was getting annoyed by it. *Big* time.

"Will you *stop—*?" she began, sitting up now, meaning to finish with *"doing that?"* and maybe adding a *"for Christ's sake!"* for emphasis. But the words died, incomplete, because what came out wasn't her voice at all, and she realized in confused alarm that he hadn't been reading her mind and she hadn't been hearing Calvin's voice all along. Or, rather, she *had.* It was just that his voice was coming out of *her* mouth.

"What the hell?" she said in Calvin's deep baritone. She lifted her hands and found they had changed, too, and were larger now, much larger, her fingers thicker, her nails shorter, her nailbeds frayed, her knuckles calloused.

Calvin's hands, she realized, and when she glanced down, she found herself wearing his tropical-print shirt, his olive-drab shorts. These were Calvin's clothes, Calvin's body parts, Calvin's *body,* but somehow—impossibly—she'd come to find herself *in it.*

"Oh, my God," she whispered and that was about the time a woman started screaming:

"Oh, my God! What the fuck? Mom! Mom, holy shit! Fuck!"

The woman's voice rose with mounting hysteria, and Barbara had dim recollection of her, a memory bobbing to the surface of an otherwise deep and murky bog inside her mind.

Melanie, I think she said her name was. Or was it Molly? No, that's not it. It was —

"Who the hell are you?" Tammy shrieked, presumably to the woman, and when Barbara turned her head, she could see them now, Tammy marching forward, her small hands balled into furious fists, her twin braids of chestnut brown hair slapping against her shoulder blades as she moved. The woman sitting on the ground, staring at her approach in something like stricken horror, had bleached blonde hair and enormous breasts threatening to overflow the top of her tight-fitting tank top. She wore leather pants and cowboy boots, and in a flash of clarity in an otherwise bewildering situation, Barbara remembered.

Marley. Her name is Marley.

"I said who the hell are you?" Tammy screeched, swinging one of her fists up, then driving it down, hitting the blonde woman, Marley, on top of the head. Like a clockwork automaton, she wrenched the other fist back, then punched Marley again, over and over. "You're not me! Why do you look like me? Why the fuck do you look like me?"

Marley yelped and threw her hands up, trying to ward off the sudden volley of blows. "Stop it," she cried. "Get off of me! Mom, help!"

Mom? Barbara thought, stunned and confused. It didn't take long to put the pieces together: the flagrant cussing, the plea for a parent in the face of imminent danger. As impossible as it was for her to now be inside her husband's body, somehow her son had likewise come to be inside of Marley's.

"Peter?" she gasped, and both Peter and Tammy swung in her direction. Only Peter was Marley now, which meant Tammy was...

"Marley?" Barbara gawked at her.

Tammy's eyes flashed, her brows crimping hotly. "What?"

"Oh, my God," Barbara moaned.

"Dad?" Peter said.

Barbara shook her head. "No, it's me, Peter. It's Mom."

Peter's eyes widened. He had mascara on now because Marley wore it, along with thick stripes of eyeliner and way too much eyeshadow.

"Mom?" he gulped. "Wh-what happened? Why do you look like Dad?"

"Mom?" Tammy turned to look at him, then swung around to face her again. "Dad? Do you mean...?" Her voice trailed off and she uttered a sharp bark of laughter. "Are you trying to tell me..." She glared at Peter. "...that you're that pimply-faced freak whose old man tried to run over my fricking dog?"

"Hey," Peter said, slitting Marley's eyes. "I'm not a freak."

"And Pops over here..." Tammy hooked a thumb at Barbara. "...is really your mom? Okay, damn." She laughed again. "This is officially messed up."

"Where is my daughter?" With a grimace, Barbara stumbled to her feet. She felt a sudden swell of panic as she realized if the person who looked like Tammy was in fact *not* Tammy, then that meant she had no idea where her daughter really was. "Where the hell is Tammy? What have you done with her?"

Marley drew back as she marched forward, but a new voice, quiet and tremulous, gave Barbara pause.

"H-here, Mommy. I'm over here."

The man sitting up behind her had introduced himself as Dr. Albert Monroe in what now seemed like a dream, when they'd pulled into a rest station in the middle of nowhere so Craig could check the GPS. They'd been the only people there: the Baxter family in the hulking wreck of an RV Craig had rented for their sad excuse for a family vacation; Marley, who'd come at them screaming before they'd even finished parking, accusing them of almost running over some mangy mutt she'd let off the leash to roam; and Dr. Monroe, middle-aged and overweight, looking like he'd just stepped out from behind the lectern of an introductory collegiate anthropology class.

He'd told us he was looking for something, waiting to see if it would appear, she recalled. *A door of some kind, didn't he say? Something he'd been studying.*

Monroe stared at Barbara now, his thinning hair sticking out in silver tufts, his eyes enormous, magnified behind the thick lenses of his glasses. His tie hung askew, and there was dirt on the front of his shirt, the lapel of his tweed jacket.

"Mommy," Tammy said from inside Dr. Monroe, and her eyes swam with sudden tears. "Mommy, I feel weird. What's happening? Where's Stanley?"

That was right about the time that Marley started to shriek, this time in terror, not anger. Flailing her arms, she danced in a careening circle, swatting at her hips.

"Something's moving," she screamed. "Oh, my God, what the fuck is moving in my—"

In her madcap fumbling, she managed to knock something out of her pocket, a small animal with black and white fur that went promptly sailing away from her, landing with a rustle near Tammy.

"Stanley!" Scrambling forward, Tammy scooped the dazed hamster in her hands and began plastering it with kisses. "Mommy! It's Stanley!"

"What…the fuck…" Marley asked, each word punctuated by labored wheezes, "…is a Stanley?"

"He's my friend," Tammy said. "I put him in my pocket, back when we were at the rest stop. I thought I'd lost him."

"You put a rodent in your pocket?" Marley sounded aghast.

Tammy glowered. "Stanley's not a rodent. He's part of the family."

"He's a rodent," Peter said drolly, which only made his sister's frown deepen.

"He's a *hamster*," she said. "And I love him. So shut up, you poop head."

"You shut up, fart breath."

"Both of you stop." There could be no denying now that these were indeed Barbara's children. Or, she realized, at least *two* of them. "Where's Olivia?" She whirled around, trying look in all directions at once. "Oh, my God, where's the baby?"

They appeared to be in the lobby of some kind of derelict hotel, with broad glass windows and the main entrance to her right, a vacant counter for checking in to her left. In between these, a dirty, debris-covered marble floor, and above, a crumbling, decaying ceiling through which tangles of leafy green vines protruded.

"Oh, God," Barbara wailed, vision blurring with tears now, her voice—Calvin's voice—growing choked with them. "Where's Olivia? Peter, Tammy, help me! Do either of you see—"

As if on cue, she heard a shrill warble as Olivia began to cry and caught sight of the floral-patterned leggings from Gymboree she'd dressed the baby in that morning, with a matching hot pink knit top with glittery, iron-on letters plastered across the front, proclaiming "Mommy Luvs Me."

And because she did—Barbara luv'd Olivia very, very much—she rushed to her, plucking the infant from behind a toppled trash can that had kept her hidden from more immediate view. Olivia had lost her pacifier, and wailed at the top of her lungs now, inconsolable, but at least she seemed to be herself, the right Barker child in the right body.

"Oh, thank God you're okay." Overwhelmed with abject relief that all of her babies were safely accounted for, Barbara smothered her with kisses. "Thank God!"

"I'm okay, too," she heard someone say. "Thanks for asking."

She'd only ever really listened to herself before in recordings, like her voicemail greeting on her cellphone, and to do so had always made her cringe because she hated the sound of her own voice. It took her a moment now to recognize it, if only because she hadn't physically spoken the words, and it took an even longer moment for her to realize the woman limping out through the open doorway of a darkened office was *her*, or at least, her body.

Startled, unnerved, she drew back. "Who…who are…?"

"It's me, Barb," her body answered, and even though the petulant expression crossed Barbara's face, it was something she recognized instantly as all-too familiar from somebody else.

"Calvin?"

You should leave him. Sheila's words floated through her mind. *He cheated on you. Men like that don't ever change. If you take him back, he'll only do it to you again.*

"Yeah, it's me," he said again. "Sorry to disappoint you." Broken glass and grit crunched beneath the soles of Barbara's wedge sandals as he staggered forward, visibly uncomfortable and struggling for balance.

"Okay, what the fuck is going on?" Marley demanded. "What is this place? What the hell happened to all of us? And where the hell is my dog?"

Apparently deciding the answer to this latter was more important than any of the former, she tromped across the foyer, cupping her hands to her mouth. "Bucky! Here, boy! Bucky, come!"

"What happened?" Calvin asked Barbara. "Last thing I remember was a bunch of swirling lights."

As he said this, Barbara remembered, too, the last bits of half-faded memories snapping abruptly into focus again.

"There was some sort of rectangle that was glowing in the air." Peter had gotten to his feet—or rather, to Marley's—and gawked at himself, clapping his hands across his leather-clad hips, the slim expanse of his waist. "I remember that. That crazy old man, he called it a door."

"I'm not crazy," Dr. Monroe said. Or at least, Barbara assumed it was Dr. Monroe inside her son's body as he stood up from behind one of the nearby check-in counters. He glanced down, and like Peter, gave himself a marveling sort of pat-down, then looked up again. "I'm not. I'm a theoretical physicist specializing in the study of quantum gravity."

"Yeah?" Having overheard this, Marley laughed. "Look in the mirror. Right now, you're a pimple-faced emo who needs a tanning bed and a haircut."

"I'm not an emo," Peter snapped. "And I don't have pimples. That's razor burn."

"Yeah." Marley awarded him a dismissive glance. "Right. And watch the hands, freak. Quit touching my boobs."

"Is everyone okay?" Dr. Monroe asked, walking toward Barbara.

"You mean, aside from the fact none of us are in the bodies we were born with? We're great," Calvin replied snidely, wobbling again. With a glare at Barbara, almost accusatory, he added, "Jesus, why did you wear these shoes?"

"Do you know what happened to us?" Barbara ignored him and addressed Monroe. "Do you know where we are?"

"And do you know how the hell we get back in our right goddamn bodies?" Marley added.

"I want to go home," Tammy whined, still cradling Stanley in her hands as she sat on the ground. "Mommy, Daddy, please, can we go home now?"

Calvin stepped forward like he meant to go to her, but Barbara beat him to it. Squatting, she held Olivia tucked in the crook of one elbow, while hooking the other around Tammy's neck, drawing her into an embrace. "It's going to be alright," she whispered. "Everything will be okay."

"We traveled through the doorway," Dr. Monroe said. "We've crossed into an alternate dimension, a universe that's parallel to the one we know as our reality. Something must have happened in the process, a quantum paradox that's resulted in the exchanging of our minds."

Calvin blinked at him. "We did *what?*"

"Told you he was crazy," Peter muttered.

"I don't care how it happened. All I want to know is how to undo it," Marley snapped. "I didn't ask to be ten years old again."

Sniffling, Tammy raised her head from Barbara's shoulder. "I'm eight."

"Whatever. You're not old enough to drink," Marley told her. "Which is exactly what I need right now — a good, goddamn stiff one. Because this is fucked up."

"You're not drinking alcohol in my daughter's body," Barbara told her with a frown.

"If I find some, I sure as hell am," Marley shot back. Whirling to Peter, she added in a snarl, "And if you touch my boobs again, kid, I'm going to kick your ass."

"Alright, everybody just stop," Calvin snapped. "No one is drinking, and no one needs to be touching anything, body parts or otherwise, at least until we figure out what's going on, and what we need to do to fix it."

You're good at that, aren't you? Barbara bit back the retort. This wonderful little family vacation had been his idea of "fixing things," only he'd been the one to break the things that needed repairing. Namely their marriage.

"*Can* we fix it?" she asked Dr. Monroe. "That glowing thing we saw, you said it was a door? Back at the rest stop, you told us you've been studying it. You know what it is, then, how it works, what it does. Right?"

She said this last as a helpless sort of plea.

"I've studied it, yes," Dr. Monroe said. "But I'm no closer to understanding how it works right now than I was fifteen years ago when I first hypothesized it. The door isn't a real door, not in the physical sense of the word. It's more of a hole, one where gravity wears through space-time itself at regular intervals, making it collapse and taking with it all the layers that separate the dimensions of existence. Like a black hole, except those exist in space. This hole exists in *space-time*."

"Regular intervals?" Barbara repeated, seized with sudden hope. "Does that mean it's going to come back? We can go through it again?"

"Oh, yes," Dr. Monroe said. "Theoretically, we can go through it as many times as we want, potentially reaching infinite points in the space-time continuum. An infinite number of dimensions."

"I don't want to reach infinity," Marley groused, "or beyond. I want to go home again — right the fuck back where we started, and with the body I started out in."

"Will going through the door again fix things?" Barbara asked. "Will it put us back the way we were?"

"Theoretically?" he said. "I believe so, yes."

"Good enough for me," Marley said. "Let me find Bucky and let's get the hell out of here."

"Where *is* here, anyway?" Calvin wondered, looking around. "This doesn't look like another dimension to me, just a rundown hotel."

"There are palm trees," Barbara observed. "And all of those vines. It looks like someplace tropical."

"Parallel dimensions can have any number of similarities to the one we know," Monroe said. "And an infinite number of differences."

"Well, wherever the hell it is, it's hot," Peter complained, gathering Marley's hair in his hands, and holding it up to expose the back of her neck. "I'm wearing leather pants. That makes it even worse."

"At least you're not wearing high heels," Calvin told him.

"They're not high heels," Barbara said with a frown.

"I'm standing six inches off the ground," he shot back. "It's like being on stilts. I can hardly balance in these things."

"They're wedges," Barbara snapped. "And they're only two inches at most. And barely even that."

"I can predict when it will come back," Dr. Monroe said. "At least, I believe I can. I have a timer set on my phone. It's in my…" He started to reach for his right hip, then realized he was in Peter's body, and glanced sheepishly at Tammy. "It's in my pocket."

"You're lucky it's not a goddamn rodent," Marley assured him.

"Here." Tammy slipped her hand into the pocket of her slacks and producing the phone. She handed it to Barbara, who in turn gave it to Dr. Monroe.

"You think it will work here?" Calvin asked with a momentary excitement that proved short-lived.

"Oh, no," Monroe said with a chuckle. "The cell service and data wouldn't, anyway, I'm sure. Even if such things exist in this dimension, the likelihood that devices from our reality could possibly be compatible are astronomically slim. But the basic computing functions, like the calculator, should still be perfectly useful."

He tapped the screen several times, both squinting and un-squinting, as if amused by the fact he clearly no longer needed glasses because he had the eyesight of a 15-

year-old boy, not an old man. "The anomaly cycles every fifteen hours," he said. "Hyper-concentrated gravity creates a bend in the fabric of space-time separating interdimensional realities. The strain from that bend eventually becomes great enough to cause an actual tear between the worlds. As the pressure from that gravitational release dissipates, the edges of the tear close again and knit whole. But the scar that's left behind, one that's punched through hundreds, if not thousands, of individual dimensions remains, and as the force of gravity continue to press against it, building pressure again, it could rupture anew at any of those places—into any of those dimensions."

"Fifteen hours?" Barbara repeated in dismay. "You mean we have to wait that long before we can leave?"

"I'm not spending another fifteen minutes in this kid's body, never mind fifteen hours," Marley declared, as if she had a choice in the matter.

"But you see, that's the beauty of space-time," Monroe said. "Time has no meaning, no relevance. We could pass through at any given point, be it an hour from the time we left, or a century before. Fifteen hours could theoretically pass in fifteen minutes—or fifteen seconds. Or even less."

Or even more, Barbara thought, keeping this to herself. She didn't want to think about the possibility of fifteen hours being the equivalent of months, years—decades, even—in whatever the hell dimension they'd stumbled into. Especially if that meant being in Calvin's body.

"Don't tell me you still love him," Sheila had told her that morning at the diner, stirring another packet of sugar into her coffee. "After everything he's done, there's no way."

"I know, I know," Barbara had said, and she'd repeated this to herself every day since then: *After everything Calvin's done, there's no way I could still love him.*

"I've worked out a formula to predict the timing of the anomaly," Monroe said, tapping some more on his phone screen. "According to my calculations, the next rift cycle should be manifesting itself in approximately…." *Tap-tap-tap-tap.* "Forty-seven minutes and thirty-eight seconds. And it will be…" Another tap, then he turned, extending his arm, pointing. "…about one hundred and fifteen yards in that direction."

"That's the length of a football field," Calvin said. "And then some."

"And we have less than an hour to get across it," Barbara said, and for a moment, they seemed to be on the exact same mental wave-length, the way they used to be when they'd first married, finishing each other's sentences, or buying matching sweatshirts. Back before he'd had an affair and she'd started searching online for divorce attorneys.

He gave her a wistful, pleading sort of look as if he'd felt it, too, and was trying yet again, albeit wordlessly, to say how sorry he was, beg for her forgiveness, but she tore her gaze away and wouldn't look at him again. "We'd…uh, better get a move on, then," she said.

"Uh-uh. No way. I'm not going anywhere without my dog." Marley crossed her arms, and when Barbara opened her mouth to argue, she added, "And I'm willing to bet you're not going anywhere without your little princess here." She swept her hands in a downward motion, indicating Tammy's body. "So, I suggest you zip your fucking lip there, Pops, and all of you help me find Bucky."

◆

"I'm beginning to hate that woman," Barbara muttered as they made their way along one of the dilapidated corridors inside the hotel.

"Me, too," Tammy said, trailing behind her. "She called Stanley a rodent."

She'd tucked the hamster into one of the pockets of Monroe's jacket, and walked now with her hand pressed against it, as if for safekeeping. They'd already wasted a good ten minutes searching for Marley's stupid mutt, by Barbara's watch, and the only thing they'd managed to do was wander aimlessly—and in vain—around the ruins of the once-posh resort.

"What do you think happened here?" Peter asked, pausing every now and again to peer into vacant rooms with open doors, or trying the handles of those doors that remained closed to see if any were unlocked. They'd discovered that most of the rooms appeared to have been hastily abandoned, with suitcases and personal belongings still strewn about inside. The hallways and stairwells were littered, too.

"I don't know," Barbara said, keeping her voice low and nearly reverent, as if they walked through the corridors of a church.

Or a cemetery, she thought with a shiver, because that's what it felt like to her, that they crept through the decaying aftermath of some kind of horrible event, something from which none of the people whose belongings they came across could have possibly survived.

There were dark brown stains on the carpeting, splattered and crusted on the walls. She tried to tell herself it was mud, not dried blood. All the windows and sliding glass doors in the rooms had been shattered, and she tried not to notice the glass always seemed to be on the inside, not scattered across the patios overlooking the dense, overgrown rainforest engulfing the resort.

Like something broke them from the outside, she thought, shuddering again. *Like it was trying to get in.*

They'd started on the garden level, then worked their way up from there as quickly as they could. Calvin had originally suggested they split up into teams, that they'd cover more ground that way, but Marley had vetoed this idea.

"There's no way in hell any of you are getting out of my sight," she'd told them. "Or leaving me behind."

Barbara could have argued that Marley needn't worry about that, because there was no way in hell she was abandoning her daughter's body. Instead, she settled for glowering at Marley as she walked ahead of them, calling out the dog's name, her voice — Tammy's voice — bouncing in haunting echo off the sun-bleached walls and broken window frames.

"This place smells weird," Tammy said. She'd tried taking off Monroe's glasses because they kept slipping down her nose, annoying her, but she'd quickly realized he was pretty much blind as a bat without them. Which meant that she, was, too, and she'd been scowling steadily ever since she'd put them back on. "Can you smell it, Mommy? It's stinky."

"I think it's all the flowers," Barbara said, because a lot of the vines that had infiltrated the crumbling hotel were of the blooming variety, a veritable rainbow of large, exotic blooms, with cloying fragrances that intermingled in the air in a thick cloud.

"Since when do flowers smell like shit?" Peter asked, earning him a warning look from Barbara.

"Watch your mouth," she said. Then, to Tammy: "Sometimes flowers that smell bad to us smell good to other things, like insects or birds, animals that help gather nectar, pollen, or seeds and spread them in the environment."

"Hey, yeah," Peter said. "There's even one kind that smells like a dead body." Another admonishing glare from Barbara and he managed to look wounded. "What? I read about it online."

Calvin turned over his shoulder to Dr. Monroe. "How much time left?"

Dr. Monroe checked his phone, then glanced at her with a grim sort of urgency she could completely relate to. "Thirty minutes, twenty-two seconds."

Again, Barbara and Calvin exchanged knowing looks. *Screw the dog,* those looks imparted. *It's time to get the hell out of Dodge and go home.*

"Hey, uh, Marley?" Calvin called, forced lightness in his voice. "We really need to start thinking about making our way toward the portal."

"*You* think about it," she replied hotly and without turning around. "I've told you already. I'm not leaving here without my dog."

"You know, there are six other people here," Barbara said, aggravated and tired of the game. "And none of us elected you the leader."

Marley stopped now and turned. There was something intimidating about having an eight-year-old child bore holes through you with her gaze, like she was imagining a million possible ways she could gut you like a fish in that moment.

"Oh, yeah?" she snarled. "Well, news flash, bitch. None of you *had* to elect me because I'm the one with the—"

As she spoke, she reached for the small of her back. All at once, that triumphant sneer wilted from the corners of her mouth, and that murderous glint in her eyes shifted to alarm.

"—gun?" Peter finished for her, and when Barbara looked, to her surprise, she found him holding a pistol with both hands, arms extended, the snub-nosed barrel aiming with wavering menace for Marley's face. "Wrong. I've got it. You had it in the back of your pants." There was a tell-tale *snact!* as he cocked the hammer. "Don't call my mom a bitch."

For a long, awkward moment, heavy silence gripped them all. Then, mustering some of her former bravado, Marley managed a snort. "What are you going to do, kid? Shoot me?"

"No." Barbara reached out, catching the gun by the barrel, easing it down. "He's not."

Peter's eyes were round with apprehension, and even though they were Marley's, she could clearly see her son behind them, his fear.

"No one is shooting anyone," Barbara said. "But we're done looking for the dog. Is that clear? We're following Dr. Monroe, and we're going to find that portal. We're going to go home. And if you don't come with us willingly, by God and all that's holy, I will pick you up by the scruff of my daughter's T-shirt and carry you the entire way."

Marley stared at her, and Barbara expected more push-back. Like Peter, however, Marley seemed to think better of any protest she might have offered. Pressing her lips together in a thin line, balling her fists in rigid defiance, she nonetheless offered a curt nod.

"Fine," she said. "Whatever." With a pointed glare in Peter's direction, she added to Barbara, *"Bitch."*

◆

"Why didn't Olivia change?" Calvin asked. They'd left the hotel grounds and started picking their way through the surrounding jungle. Without their cell phones or a compass to guide them, they were left to trust Monroe's sense of direction, which he seemed to obtain by occasionally glancing up at the sky and noting the position of the sun, or by licking his fingertip and pointing it skyward as if in exclamation.

"All the rest of us swapped bodies," Calvin continued. He and Barbara had been taking turns carrying the baby—or rather, Barbara had been carrying Olivia since they'd started the search and had only just now passed her off to Calvin despite his grumbling protests. "But she's still the same."

"Maybe she swapped with Stanley," Peter remarked and when Barbara scowled, he said, "What? Like we could tell the difference? It's not like either of them talk or anything."

"Don't be stupid," Calvin told him, but Barbara found herself looking at Olivia now, asleep in Calvin's arms, and couldn't help but wonder. After all, she realized, Peter *did* have a point.

"Where's Stanley?" she whispered to Tammy.

"Right here," Tammy replied, patting her pocket.

"Keep him safe," Barbara said. *Just in case.*

"Once the anomaly, door, or whatever it is opens again, how long will it last?" Calvin said to Monroe. "How much time do we have to cross through it?"

"According to the computer models I've run in my lab, the rift remains open for thirteen minutes and forty-five seconds. Then all of the dimensional layers collapse and seal themselves off again."

"'According to the computer models?'" Calvin frowned. "What does that mean?"

"I've never actually timed it," Monroe said. "The anomaly, I mean. I've never seen it until today."

Calvin drew to a halt. "I thought you knew about this thing. You studied it, you said."

"I've known it's theoretically possible," Monroe said. "And I've tracked electromagnetic readings that corroborate the probability that the rift occurs. But physically studying it? No. I've never been able to confirm its existence until today."

"Then how the hell do you know it's going to get us home again?" Calvin demanded.

Caught off guard by the sudden sharpness in his voice, Monroe blinked and sputtered. "Well, I...I just...that is to say..."

"He doesn't," Marley said, hands planted on her hips. "Do you, Doc? You have no fucking clue where we're going to end up when we go back through that door."

"Now that...that isn't..." Monroe began, bright red splotches of anxious color blooming in his cheeks, a sheen of perspiration suddenly glossing his brow. "I didn't say that. When the door is open, it's open across *every* dimension. It's just a matter of finding the correct exit point to get back to our reality."

"Yeah?" Now Calvin matched Marley's obstinate stance. "How do we do that?"

"I...I just...I don't know. It's all been purely academic until today. I never actually imagined that I would find the rift, never mind go *through* it."

"So you're saying even if we find this fucking thing, there's the chance we won't end up back where we belong at all?" Calvin demanded.

"Or in the right bodies?" With a cackle, Marley threw up her hands. "That's great. That's just fucking great. Next time around, maybe I'll end up inside of Pops here, or even—"

From somewhere nearby, off to their right, they heard a dog begin to bark, a thick, guttural, urgent sound that reverberated among the tree trunks and tangled vines, bouncing off the canopy of palm fronds and leaves overhead.

"That's Bucky!" Marley turned, her eyes flown wide, her mouth falling open in a joyous, gaping O. "Bucky She took off running, ducking and shoving through the flowers and vines, disappearing into the dense underbrush. "Bucky!" they heard her shout. "Bucky, here, boy! Here, Buck!"

"Marley, wait!" Peter rushed after her, headlong and heedless.

"Peter, no—!" Barbara cried out in alarm. Calvin had the baby, so she started running after their son, seized with sudden panic at the thought of losing him—and Tammy, too, or at least her body—in all that overgrown foliage. "Peter, goddamn it, come back!"'

"Mommy!" Tammy bawled from behind her.

Of course Calvin made no move to follow, never mind help. He wouldn't have, even if he'd still been in his own body, not hers, and wearing Air Jordans instead of strappy sandals. Sheila was right, Barbara realized; she should have left him. He was so goddamn useless. If this entire wretched experience taught her anything, then maybe it was that she needed to get some balls—figuratively, next time, instead of literally—and divorce his worthless ass.

"Peter," she shouted, low-lying limbs and wayward branches snagging in her hair, slapping and stinging her face. Vines tangled around her ankles, threatening to trip her with every step, and she danced and stumbled through them, trying to see far enough ahead to find her son. She could still hear Bucky barking like crazy, and Marley calling its name. She tried to let the sounds guide her.

"Peter," she cried. "Peter, wait!"

All at once, Bucky yiped, a horrible, agonized sound. Barbara staggered to a halt, gasping for breath, her eyes flown wide. She had no idea what could have made the dog utter a cry like that, but in that moment, she thought of the suspicious stains that might have been blood on the hotel carpets, and all the broken windows as if something—or *somethings*—had battered their way inside.

"*Bucky!*" Marley screamed, her voice filled with the same sort of panic that Barbara had felt back inside the hotel, when she'd realized she couldn't find Olivia. "Bucky, no, no, no! Let go of my dog! *Let go of my goddamn dog!*"

The booming report of a gunshot resounded through the trees, and that more than anything galvanized Barbara back into motion. She'd meant to take the gun away from Peter back at the hotel but realized now that she'd been caught up in the tension of the moment and forgotten. Which meant…

"Peter!" She started to run again, bursting through the brush and into a small clearing. Here, ferns grew in broad, vernal fronds nearly as high as her waist. She saw Peter ahead of her, still holding the gun, albeit loosely in his hand, his arm dangling impotently at his side.

Marley stood beside him, both with their backs to Barbara. Neither turned at her clumsy, rushing entrance — and once she saw what was in front of them, she found she couldn't blame them. Not one damn bit.

An enormous bulb towered at the opposite side of the clearing, some kind of monstrous plant that stood at least ten feet in height. A tangled network of vines framed it, some as thick in circumference as one of Barbara's thighs. These were moving, she realized in shock and horror, squirming and thrashing like a nest of anacondas, rising into the air with menacing purpose, the undersides hooked with what appeared to be thorns, each as long and as big around as her thumb.

One of those barbed tentacles had grabbed hold of Bucky, the thorns tearing into the poor dog's flesh. Bucky struggled to try and get free, even as the movement caused the barbs to dig even more deeply. The dog whined and howled, its eyes round and frantic, its paws scrabbling vainly for purchase as it was dragged backwards.

The bulb split apart along unseen seams, opening at Bucky's approach as if in anticipation, the thick green leaflets peeling back and drooping to reveal bright fuchsia beneath, gigantic flower petals that, when fully unfurled, spanned at least fifteen feet across. In the center, framed by the petals, Barbara saw something unexpected and hideous — a leviathan-like mouth, wide open and gnashing, a gaping maw ringed with layer after concentric layer of jagged teeth. A stench like a body that had been floating face-down in a swamp it her, and Barbara stumbled back, gagging.

"Let go of my dog!" Marley shrieked, her voice choked with sobs. She grabbed for the gun, and in his shock and terror, Peter didn't try to stop her. She snatched it from his grasp, then began to fire wildly, her shots smashing into the ground, ricocheting off nearby trees. A vine lashed out, snapping around her leg, whipping it out from beneath her. She fell onto her back with a breathless cry, then screamed as it jerked her across the ground. More vines encircled her legs and arms as she thrashed. She managed to flip herself onto her belly, then clawed at the ground, her fingers digging fierce trenches through the dirt as she slid past.

"Help!" she wailed.

"Leave her alone!" Peter cried, though whether rushing to Marley's defense, or seeing only his sister in his stark terror, Barbara couldn't be sure. He dove after Marley, arms outstretched, catching her by the hand.

"Mom," he pleaded. "Mom, help me! Come on!"

Barbara scrambled to his side, coiling her fingers around Marley's wrist and hanging on for dear life. She couldn't believe how much force they fought against, how impossibly strong the vines were. Even with Calvin's size on her side, his larger hands and broader shoulders, his heavier frame to anchor them in place, she could feel herself losing her grip, Marley getting dragged away from them.

"Don't let go," Marley begged. "Oh, God, please don't let me go!"

"We...won't...!" Peter gasped, even though Barbara knew damn good and well it was about to become a promise neither could keep. Looking around wildly for anything she could use as a weapon, she spied something on Peter's belt: a black leather sheath affixed to the strap, with a black hilt protruding from the top. Marley noticed it, too, and her eyes widened all the more.

"My knife," she said. "Hurry! Get it! Help me!"

Barbara tried to reach for it with one hand but had to catch hold of Marley's wrist again as the vines tried to yank her away. "Can you reach it?" she asked Peter, but each time he tried, the vines would somehow sense their resistance slackening and pull all the more, forcing him to abandon his efforts or lose his grasp.

"What are we going to do?" he cried, then as another vine shot out, coiling around his leg, he began to scream. "Mom! Oh, shit, it's got me! Jesus fuck! *Mom!*"

"Don't let go," she heard a familiar voice say in her ear—her own voice. Looking over her shoulder, she saw Calvin standing there. He'd followed them somehow through the trees, making his way despite the sundress and sandals slowing him down. His face—Barbara's face—was riddled with scratches, bruises, and scrapes, his mouth set in a thin line of grim determination.

Bending down, he wrenched Marley's knife loose from Peter's belt, then drove it down in a swift arc, burying the blade in the thick vine that clung to Peter's leg. Working furiously, he began hacking at the stalk, until at last, it scuttled back in wounded recoil. Bright green slime, viscous and rancid, trailed behind it. Scrambling to Marley, Calvin began sawing at the vines wrapped around her legs, pausing only to swing and stab at vines darting toward them, trying to reclaim their lost holds.

"Pull her back," he told Barbara and Peter as at last, he managed to cut Marley free. "Pull her back, get her up!"

"Bucky," Marley pleaded. "Please, you have to help my dog!"

Calvin looked helplessly torn, then Peter snatched the knife, ripping it out of his father's grasp.

"You guys run," he said. "I'll get Bucky and catch up."

"No—" Barbara cried, but it was too late. Peter had already spun around and rushed back toward the dog.

"Get up," Calvin said, getting an arm around her and yanking. "Barbara, for God's sake, get up!"

"No, we can't leave Peter!" she screamed.

"We're not," he screamed back. "I'll help him, goddamn it. You two get out of here! Run!" When neither Barbara nor Marley moved, he waved his arms at them, a violent, shooing motion. *"Go!"*

They began to run, not daring to look behind them, both bolting through the trees again. Within moments, Barbara felt someone catch her by the hand, and she turned, surprised to see Calvin sprinting alongside her. She saw Peter close behind, his cheeks flushed, his face shiny with sweat as he carried Bucky in his arms.

Beyond him, she could hear thunderous crashes and heavy snapping of tree limbs, as if the carnivorous plant had pulled up its roots and somehow gave chase. The four of them ran until Barbara's lungs burned with desperate exertion, until Calvin's shirt felt sweat-soaked and clung to her like a second skin. They made it back to the place where it all had started, back at the ruins of the once-grand resort, the crumbling hotel lobby where they found Dr. Monroe and Tammy waiting for them, little Olivia sound asleep in Monroe's arms.

"Oh, thank God," he exclaimed, with a breathless sort of relief that clearly suggested he hadn't expected see any of them alive ever again.

"Mommy!" Tammy rocketed forward, bursting into new tears as she plowed into Barbara, big enough in Dr. Monroe's form to send Barbara floundering off balance. "Mommy, you're bleeding!"

"It's okay, sweetheart," Barbara said, hugging her fiercely. "I'm alright. We're all okay."

As she held her daughter, she turned her gaze toward her husband, as if seeing him for the very first time. If she hadn't witnessed what had happened, what he'd done with her very own eyes, she would have sworn it was impossible, would have laughed and said there was no way, he didn't have it in him. Calvin Baxter would never fight off a giant, man-eating flower.

"You saved my dog," Marley said to Peter, her voice winded and weary as she stared at him in something like wonder. He set Bucky down, and the dog wagged its tail, tongue lolling even as it wobbled for balance. With a choked cry, Marley knelt and locked her arms around Bucky's neck, burying her face in the dog's thick fur. When she looked up again at Peter, her eyes swam with tears. "Thank you."

Peter tried to shrug it off. "No problem," he mumbled, even as color bloomed in his cheeks, almost shyly.

◆

"How much time is left?" Calvin asked grimly, holding up a machete they'd found in a gardening shed on the hotel grounds.

"Until the portal disappears?" Monroe asked, glancing at his watch. "Eleven minutes."

They were too late to catch it as it opened again, but if they could still reach it before it closed once more, they could get through. They'd raided the resort for any semblance of weapons they could find: the machete, along with an assortment of butcher knives discovered in the kitchen, and a can of hairspray along with a dented Zippo lighter. Marley's gun was gone, lost in the woods, but Calvin had given the hunting knife back to her and she held it now with a fierce sort of familiarity that made Barbara wonder what sort of life she'd had before their paths had all crossed.

From one of the third-floor balconies, they could see the jungle below, and past it, a white stretch of sandy beach with the turquoise expanse of an anonymous sea beyond.

"The door will manifest there," Monroe said.

"On the beach?" Marley said. "You mean we have to get all the way through the jungle to reach it? There's no way."

From their vantage, they could see things moving among the trees, leafy crowns shivering, palm crowns swaying, and the air filled with rustles, snaps, and crackles. It sounded like an army closing in on them, and Barbara had a sinking feeling that's exactly what it was. One predatory plant alone hadn't caused all that damage to the hotel and its occupants. God only knew how many of them were out there, aware of their presence now, and hungry for blood.

"We're never going to make it," Marley said.

"Don't talk like that," Peter said.

"Peter's right. We stick together, have each other's backs," Calvin said. "No one gets taken. No one gets left behind."

"I'm scared," Tammy whimpered. She'd taken Stanley out of her pocket and held him up to her face now, nuzzling his fur with her nose. "Stanley is, too."

"It's alright." Barbara tried to smile, to somehow reassure her, even though she was scared, too. Shitless, in fact.

They left the hotel, moving in tight formation, with Calvin at the front of the line, Barbara and Marley bringing up the rear. Peter carried Bucky again, because even though they'd done their best to bind the wounds where the thorns had cut, the poor dog still couldn't do more than hobble a few limping steps before crumpling. Marley had tried to pick it up, but in Tammy's body, she'd been neither big nor strong enough to manage.

"I'll take him," Peter had offered, and again, she'd looked at him as if he were an arc angel or some other celestial being, descending from the heavens with golden sunbeams shooting out of his ass.

Monroe kept to the middle, carrying Olivia across his chest in a makeshift sling they'd fashioned out of bed sheets. Calvin wielded the machete, clearing their path through the trees, while Barbara kept a look out, holding the half-empty can of Rave Extra Hold in one trembling hand, the lighter in the other.

"If anything comes at us, you torch it," Calvin had told her.

Despite all of the noise they'd heard from the hotel, the jungle lay eerily still and quiet now. It occurred to Barbara just how strange it was, and how she hadn't noticed until just then. There were no birds singing, no insects chirping, no frogs chirruping. There wasn't even a breeze to stir leaves overhead. Nothing but silence, again as heavy and smothering as a shroud.

"Where did they go?" Marley whispered. Calvin shushed her from over his shoulder, but she ignored him, speaking instead to Barbara. "You saw them, didn't you? When we were back in the hotel. This place was filled with…things. Moving things."

"Yeah." Barbara nodded. "I saw them."

"So where did they go?" Marley tightened her grip on the knife hilt, eyes darting nervously about.

As if on cue, Tammy suddenly uttered a startled squawk, then crashed to the ground, her feet jerked out from beneath her.

"Mommy—!" she cried, then she whipped off into the underbrush, snatched at lightning speed by a hidden tangle of vines.

"Tammy!" Barbara shouted, and they all sprang after her, with Calvin swinging his blade wildly, scattering leaves and limbs in all directions. Ahead of them, through the trees,

Barbara saw a flash of fuchsia and caught a pungent whiff of decay.

"There!" she screamed, raising the can of hairspray in one hand, and snapping the Zippo open with the other. Depressing the nozzle, she spun the lighter's flint wheel, sparking a sudden flame. "Let go of my baby!"

A stream of fire, blue-gold and blazing, shot out of the can, searing a line in midair. The flames struck the flower nearly dead center, setting it instantly alight. Calvin had his hands beneath Tammy's arms the instant the vines turned her loose, yanking her upright and dragging her away from the plant's reach. As it burned, Barbara could hear a hideous, horrible, gargling sound, like a strangled scream, and its vines flailed wildly.

Another flash of bright pink as another bud opened, this time on their right. Marley uttered a shriek as a swell of vines came at her, then Calvin rushed to her side, both of them swinging their blades, driving the plants back.

"Go," Calvin shouted. "Barbara, grab Tammy! Come on! Go, go!"

They ran like hell, hacking their way through vines, past dozens upon dozens of flowers. By the time they reached the beach, their clothes were torn, their bodies bruised and battered, all of them limping, bleeding, panting for ragged breath. Behind them, they could hear the plants moving again, more vines rushing eagerly toward them, the proverbial dinner bell having been rung.

"Where…is it…?" Barbara gasped, shielding her eyes from the sun's glare with the blade of her hand, squinting against the sting of blood. "Where's the door? Can anybody see it?"

"How much time do we have?" Calvin asked, as they all turned frantically this way and that, staring up one stretch of the shoreline, then the other.

"Three minutes, thirty seconds," Monroe said.

"Where the hell is it?" Marley cried.

"I don't know," he said, fumbling with his phone again. "I...I don't understand. It should be right here. Let me work the calculation again..."

"We don't have time for that," Marley exclaimed. "Those fucking things are coming. We have to get out of here, right now!"

"There! I see it!" Tammy pointed toward the water, and they all turned to look. At first, Barbara saw no more than a thin stripe of light hovering above the sand. Then she realized Tammy was right; it was the door, only they were seeing it from the side, not the front.

"Mommy, there," Tammy said, pointing again. "Do you see?"

Barbara caught her hand, squeezed it fiercely. "I see it, honey."

"Thank God," Marley said.

"Let's get the fuck out of here!" Peter had set Bucky down, but reached for the dog now, meaning to pick it up again.

Marley grinned. "You said it, kid. I've never been more ready in all my—"

Her voice cut short, and she uttered a sharp cry as a vine whipped around her neck from behind. "Oh, shit—!"

she gulped, then choked as she flew back toward the tree line.

"Marley!" Abandoning the dog, Peter ran after her, the heels of his cowboy boots kicking up clods of sand with every stride. He threw himself at her, wrapping his arms around her waist. *"Dad!"* he screamed. "Dad, help!"

Calvin rushed toward him, still brandishing the machete. While Peter held onto Marley for dear life, prying at the vine, loosening its chokehold on her, Calvin brought the blade of the machete down, hacking at the vine to free her. More of that pungent slime splattered, until at last the plant scrabbled back, uttering a high-pitched chittering sound, like a pissed-off cicada.

"Are you okay?" Peter asked Marley, wide-eyed and flushed. "Oh, Jesus, your neck! You're bleeding."

She winced as she gingerly touched the cuts along her throat where the thorns had pierced her skin. "I'm alright. It's nothing." With a frown, she slapped him. "What the hell's wrong with you? The door's right there. You should've let it take me."

"No one gets taken," Peter said as he stood, then offered his hand to her. "No one left behind. Remember?"

With a smile, Calvin tousled his hair. "That's right, son."

"Yeah, well, you're both still dumbasses," Marley muttered as Peter helped her up. She cut a glance at him and smiled. "Especially you."

"Fifty-three seconds!" Monroe cried. "Everybody, hurry! We have to get to the door!"

They ran together down the beach until they found themselves facing the psychedelic mass of light and color swirling beyond the glowing threshold. Instead of going through it, however, they all froze on the edge of the surf, staring between the doorway and each other in obvious apprehension.

"Are you sure about this?" Calvin asked Monroe.

"That it will take us home again? No." Monroe shook his head. "It's impossible to tell. Not with any certainty."

"Who gives a fuck?" Marley said. "If we stay here, we're dead meat. And I mean literally. Anyplace has to be better."

She stepped forward but paused when Peter caught her by the shoulder. "I'll go first," he said. Then, with color in his cheeks again, he added hastily, "I mean…just in case, you know. It could be dangerous or something."

The corner of her mouth hooked in a smile. "How about we go together, then? We can look out for each other."

They stepped through the portal side by side, with Peter carrying Bucky again, and the lights swallowed them whole. Monroe went next, handing Olivia off to Calvin. Before ducking through the doorway, he glanced back and offered a sheepish sort of smile.

"See you on the other side," he said, then he was gone.

"Alright, baby, your turn." Barbara looked at Tammy and smiled. "Have you got Stanley?"

Tammy nodded, reaching into her pocket and pulled out the squirming hamster.

"Tell him not to be scared," Barbara said. "And don't you be, either, alright? I'm right behind you."

"And Daddy, too?" Tammy asked.

Barbara glanced at Calvin.

You should leave him, Sheila had told her. *Men like that don't ever change.*

Only Calvin had. More than just his body, something inside of him had changed, she realized. For the better.

"How about we all go through at the same time?" she suggested, offering him her hand. He blinked at her, as if in surprise, and not for the first time that day, she found herself remembering why she'd fallen in love with him in the first place. "That way we can face whatever's out there together."

He slipped his fingers through hers. "Alright, then," he told her. "Together."

She held on tight as the portal drew them into it, its brilliant light enveloping them, whispering the word over and over in her mind, holding onto it like a mantra: *Together.*

Beware The Grindlewog

"You had one job, man," David said, aiming the video camera and its light down at a cast iron grating on the floor. On his hands and knees, trying to angle the flashlight on his phone to see better, Adam glanced up and scowled.

"No shit," he snapped. "Will you hold that thing still so I can see?"

"I'm trying. Your head's in the way."

"You're not recording this, are you?" Adam asked, his frown deepening.

"Yeah, right. Like ten years from now, Mark's going to want to look at videos of his best man after he dropped the wedding rings down a vent."

"Fuck you. It was an accident."

The ceremony was due to begin in less than three hours. They were supposed to be getting ready so the photographer could take pictures once the bridal party arrived. Adam hadn't finished putting on his tuxedo yet; he'd just shrugged his way into the jacket when the rings had fallen out of his pocket, bouncing off the floor with a light clatter, then tumbling through the grate into darkness below.

"I can't see shit." With a frustrated growl, Adam hooked his fingers through the rust-pocked iron grid and gave a useless tug. "This isn't a vent. It's a shaft or something that goes way down. There's a dirt floor at the bottom. Must be the basement."

They were in a quaint little church dedicated to Saint Jude Thaddeus in the village of Bledington, England, about three hours northeast of London. The town was tucked among the pastoral hills of the Cotswold district of Gloucester, surrounded by equally charming little communities with names like Stow-on-the-Wold and Chipping Norton. St. Jude's, as it was called, had originally been constructed in the 12th century.

"Churches this old don't have basements," David said. "They have catacombs, underground crypts where people used to bury their dead.

"I don't care what it's called," Adam said, standing. "We have to find a way down there."

"*We* don't have to do shit," David said. "*You* dropped the rings."

"But I need your help. The light on your camera's way better than mine."

"And it's only got about a half hour left on the battery. I need to plug it in to charge before the ceremony starts."

"There isn't going to be a ceremony without those rings," Adam pleaded, and with a sigh, David relented.

"Alright. But you owe me, man. Big time."

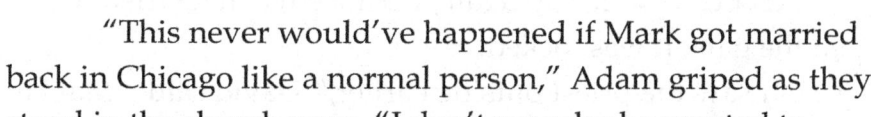

"This never would've happened if Mark got married back in Chicago like a normal person," Adam griped as they stood in the church nave. "I don't see why he wanted to have the wedding in this moldy dump in the first place."

"Because Sophie's family has lived in this area for generations. She got baptized in this church. And it's not a dump—it's medieval."

Adam looked briefly surprised that David would know this, then laughed. "That's right. I almost forgot. You two used to date or something, right?"

David managed a strained smile. "Right."

He and Sophie had been friends during their senior year of high school. She'd transferred as an exchange student from Great Britain and after graduation, when she returned to England, they'd stayed connected through social media. She'd even returned to America while in college to visit, and that's how she'd met David's roommate Mark, now her soon-to-be-husband. It had been pretty much love at first sight between them, which had broken David's heart. Not because he disliked Mark—far from it. But he'd harbored a crush on Sophie for years, one he'd never had the courage to own up to.

Now it was too late.

"What time is it?" Adam asked, and when he glanced at his phone to check, he muttered "shit!" beneath his breath. "The photographer will be here soon. We have to hurry."

Toward the back of the sanctuary, a shallow alcove had been gated off. Here, they found a staircase leading down through a dark, narrow opening in the stone floor.

"Shit," Adam said again, because when he tried to open the gate, it was locked.

"I saw the priest outside earlier," David said. "Maybe we can ask him to—"

Adam shoved against the metal bars. The iron was old, and even this quick bit of pressure knocked the tumblers out of place, releasing the lock. With a screech of scraping metal, the gate gave way.

"Are you nuts?" David looked around in alarm. "This church is like a thousand years old! You can't just—"

"No one's going to know." Adam was already making his way down the steps. "Come on."

At the bottom of the stairs, they found the passage blocked again, this time by a large wooden door. Despite its obvious age, it looked heavy and solid, like something that would mark the entrance to a castle dungeon filled with medieval torture devices. Adam gave an experimental push, but it, too, was locked.

"Let's go find the priest," David said. "He's got to have a key."

"There isn't time for that." Adam pushed his shoulder against the door. The thick wood creaked, but held its ground and with another frown, Adam stepped back to give himself some momentum.

"Stop," David said, but Adam ignored him, rushing at the door. Another groan of metal and wood, but still the lock held. Adam rammed it again, then again, and just when David was sure the racket was going to draw attention, the door unexpectedly swung open. Adam stumbled forward, off balance and clumsy, then managed to reclaim his footing.

"Jesus," David exclaimed. "Would you stop busting everything? We could've just asked someone to unlock it."

"We don't have time. I told you. If Mark finds out I lost the rings, he's going to freak. The quicker we find the damn things, the better."

"Yeah, but—"

"This is his big day," Adam said. "I don't want to let him down."

Like you did. He didn't add this out loud, but then again, he didn't need to. After all, Mark had originally invited David to be the best man. In fact, he and Sophie had asked together.

"We never would've met if it hadn't been for you," Mark had said, and David remembered staring down at Mark's hand—or more specifically, Mark holding Sophie's hand as he'd spoken, their fingers intertwined, making it hard to tell where one of them ended and the other began.

"Come on, turn the camera light on." Adam fished his phone from his pocket, then thumbed on his flashlight. "Let's just do this and get out of here."

David followed reluctantly. He'd never been in a crypt before, had only ever seen pictures of the ones beneath Paris, where the walls were decorated with skulls and bones arranged in elaborate, morbid mosaics. Sophie had told him no one had been buried in the catacombs beneath St. Jude's for over a century, that it had been a bomb shelter for residents from nearby Bledington during Nazi air raids in World War II. From the looks of things as he panned the camera, no one had been down there since.

He didn't see any bones, only stone sarcophagi lining recesses and shelves along the walls. Even so, he couldn't escape an eerie sensation, like he was being watched. The air felt damp and cold, a pervasive chill stealing through his clothes, making him shiver.

"I think it's over here," Adam was saying, heading toward where a spear of light filtered down through a shaft in the ceiling.

David started to follow but paused as he noticed strange carvings along one of the nearby walls: grotesque figures with diminutive bodies and oversized heads, their faces twisted into snarling, sneering masks of agony or anguish. What looked like poetry or a nursery rhyme had been inscribed above them in the stone:

> *Beware the Grindlewog, my friend*
> *Most foul of man or beast!*
> *For if your path should cross with them*
> *Upon your flesh, they shall feast.*

What the hell was a grindlewog? It sounded like something out of a Harry Potter book. *I'll have to ask Sophie later,* he thought. *Maybe she'll know.*

"Get over here and help, damn it." Adam spun in a helpless circle, shining his flashlight toward the floor. "I don't see the rings!"

"Relax," David said, turning away from the weird verse. "They didn't sprout legs and walk off."

But after a good ten minutes of searching, there was still no sign.

"What the fuck?" Adam cried, now shrill with panic.

"Are you sure this is where you dropped them?" David asked, and they both looked toward the ceiling. "Maybe it was a different shaft."

"You think?" Adam said, willing to grasp at any straw. "Okay, yeah, maybe. That makes sense. But then where...?" His voice faded as further down the corridor, he glimpsed another hint of sunshine seeping down from the floor above. "Over there! That's got to be it."

Without waiting for David, he took off, the beam from his phone's flashlight bouncing off the walls. Just as David moved to follow, he heard a low creak of metal from behind them, followed by a sharp, heavy clang.

Oh, shit.

When they entered the catacombs, they'd left the door standing open, yet he saw now that it had swung shut again.

David hurried back and pulled on the handle, but it didn't budge. "Hey, uh, Adam?" he called, turning around. "I think we might be..."

...in trouble, he meant to say.

"Adam?"

The crypt lay empty as far as the light from his video camera could reach.

"Adam? Where are you?" With a frown, he headed back down the catacombs. "We've got a problem, man, come on. Get out here."

As he panned the light, he noticed more of those creepy little figures carved along the walls, and more of the strange verses accompanying them:

They dwell in dark, forgotten places,
where names are long since dead.
Shadows shroud their gaunt, pale faces,
as within darkness do they tread.

What the hell? he thought, and he might have laughed had he not been so unnerved, or if it seemed like a joke. Instead, the words felt ominous to him, less like a children's rhyme and more like a warning.

"Adam?" he called again. "Damn it, I'm serious. The door closed and it's locked again. Quit—" He heard the crunch of splintering plastic underfoot and drew back, startled to discover he'd stepped on Adam's phone. When he stooped to pick it up, he saw something dark and wet across the case.

Is that blood?

All at once, the camera light dimmed and a red warning light flashed on the view finder display; the battery was down to the last fifteen percent of its charge.

Shit, he thought, because that was his only source of light. If it ran out of juice before he could find a way out…

No. He gave his head a little shake. *Don't go there.*

He'd call one of the other groomsmen for help. They'd laugh their asses off for sure, and neither he nor Adam would likely live it down, but at least they'd be out of that weird fucking crypt. When he reached for his pocket, however, he bit back a groan, remembering he'd left his phone upstairs.

"Damn it," he muttered, looking again at Adam's, and what looked like blood splattered on the case.

Don't be stupid. Of course it's not blood.

With a wince, he picked up the phone, but when he turned it over, he saw the screen had cracked down the center. Even though he tried tapping, swiping, and pressing on it, nothing happened.

"Damn it," he said again, because now the camera battery was down to twelve percent and draining fast, the light dimming by the second. "Adam? Come on, this isn't funny anymore."

He tried to tell himself that was all this was, a practical joke Adam was playing, maybe his way of getting even with David for not agreeing to be Mark's best man.

"You really hurt his feelings," he'd told David before they left for London, and David had sputtered in protest, offering the same lame excuses he'd given both Mark and

Sophie. "Seriously. You're his best friend. This is supposed to be your job."

"Come on, Adam," David shouted again. "Quit screwing around and get out here!"

His voice had taken on a shrill edge, and he struggled to tamp down his growing panic. Think, he told himself. The camera belonged to Mark; he'd bought it before leaving the States, and along the flight from New York to London, he'd showed it off to David.

"It's even got a low-light setting," he'd said. "Like night vision. See this switch here? Flip it, and you can shoot footage in the dark."

Would that use less battery power? David wasn't sure. Tipping the camera to the side, he found the switch near the base, but hesitated.

"I'm almost out of battery life on the camera, so I'm turning it off now," he called to Adam, trying to muster a bravado that he didn't feel. "Have fun trying to find the rings in the dark, asshole."

Closing his eyes and gritting his teeth, he flipped the switch, plunging himself into immediate darkness. When he opened his eyes, the view didn't change, the blackness still impenetrable and terrifying.

From his left, he heard the sudden scuffle of something moving in the dirt, close enough to startle him.

What was that?

With a yelp, David scrambled sideways, dropping the camera in surprise. He heard it hit the ground—*shit!*—and fumbled to find it, pawing blindly, his heart an audible tympany in his ears. His outstretched fingers slapped against the camera, and he seized it, clutching with both hands like he might a belay line.

It must've been a rat. He began to feel along the base of the camera to find the night vision button. *Just a rat. It had to be...*

"I-I'm going back to bang on the door," he said, snapping on the camera's low-light mode. "People will be coming in soon, so someone's bound to hear me. If you're done messing around, come help."

No answer. Through the viewfinder, he watched the world bloom into sudden, bright detail as if cast in the glare of a megawatt spotlight. He immediately turned to his left, the direction in which he'd heard the scuffle, but saw nothing there. Slowly, hesitantly, he built up his nerve and began panning the camera, letting the infrared light illuminate everything onscreen in eerie glow. On the ground, he saw a trail of black splotches, something splattered in the dirt.

Blood, he realized, unable to deny it now or push it aside, no matter how much he wanted to. *Blood, THAT'S BLOOD.*

The trail meandered down the corridor ahead of him before fading from view, and was it just his imagination, or were those scuff marks in the dirt, too, like something had been dragged along in the same direction as the blood?

Not something, he realized in mounting horror. Someone.

He heard another scrabbling sound, this time from his right, and whirled.

"Wh-who's there? Adam?"

Through the camera, he caught a blur of movement against the backdrop of shadows that almost instantly disappeared.

"I said, who's there?"

More rustles came from all sides now, like small feet pattering, and the panic that had been rising in him steadily came now to a sudden, strangling head.

David bolted for the stairs. He could hear them giving chase, those same light, swift footsteps in the dirt behind him — like an entire herd of rats — and when he reached the door, he fell against it, beating with his fist. "Help!" he cried. "Hey, someone, anyone! Help!"

He looked over his shoulder, but there was only that impregnable darkness and the footsteps rushing closer, nearly upon him. Pressing his back against the door, he raised the camera. It rattled as his hand shook, the zoom lens spinning, struggling to focus. Through the viewfinder, he saw them: dozens of tiny figures scrambling toward him. They clung, spider-like, to the crypt walls and alcoves, and he realized what he'd mistaken for carvings earlier had been these creatures all along — like children, emaciated and nude, their spindly arms and legs preternaturally elongated, their skulls smooth and hairless. They all had enormous black eyes, and hundreds of needle-like teeth, their grins as hideous and strained as David's had been when Mark asked him to be his best man.

"I don't know," he'd said, trying to tactfully decline. "That kind of thing's not for me. You should ask Adam."

I should've said yes, David realized as he glimpsed the words inscribed on the nearby wall—a warning, he understood too late. One that, like Mark's invitation, he should have heeded, because if he had, things would have likely turned out much, much different.

> *Beware the Grindlewog, my friend*
> *Most foul of man or beast!*
> *For if your path should cross with them*
> *Upon your flesh, they shall feast.*

He could see them now, the grindlewog, with their ghoulish smiles as they reached for him during those last, fleeting moments of the camera battery's life.

And his own.

The Devil You Know

"What if I said you could have all the money in the world?" Robert asked from beside Elizabeth in bed. They'd finished having sex a short time earlier and both lay winded and flushed with afterglow.

"I'd say what's the catch?" Elizabeth lifted her hand in the air, admiring the way the dim light glinted off the facets in her six-carat diamond engagement ring. She'd wanted something *huge*, she'd told Robert, and he'd obliged. The damn thing was so big it didn't even look real, more like a plastic knock-off out of a gumball machine so little girls could play pretend.

"All the money in the world," she repeated with a dubious frown. "And I can spend as much as I want?"

He nodded. "On anything you want. Whenever you want to."

"Then, yeah," she said. "I'd ask what's the catch? There has to be one. There always is."

He watched her for a moment, a soft smile playing at the corners of his lips. "You only get thirty years to spend it."

Elizabeth frowned. "Why?"

He shrugged. "That's the rule."

"What happens after thirty years are up?"

"Then it's someone else's turn."

With a thoughtful frown, she looked up at the play of light and shadows across the popcorn ceiling of their motel room. "And...what? I go back to being poor again?"

"No," he said quietly. "You die."

She considered this a moment while he played with her hair, twisting a strand around his finger, then sliding it loose over and over.

"I'd take it," she said finally. "I mean, what the hell. Thirty years is a long time. By then, I'll practically be old. What else would I have to live for?" With an impish grin, she first sat up, then flopped over, landing on top of him, her boobs crushed against his chest. "Are you offering me that? All the money in the world?"

"Maybe," he said with a smile.

"And what's in it for you?" she asked, wriggling against him, making his smile widen, his cock twitch between them.

"Nothing." Robert caught her by the back of the head, spreading his fingers through her hair, pulling her against him. He kissed her hard, and as they drew apart, Elizabeth could see herself reflected in the dark pools of his irises. "Just the pleasure of your company."

When she met Robert Mapother, he'd seemed the proverbial Prince Charming to her Cinderella, riding to the rescue if not on a white horse, then at least in a silver Bentley. At that time, she'd been scraping a meager living by shaking her ass at a strip club called The Cat's Meow. The lounge had a big neon sign out in front, the kind where some of the bulbs lit up while others darkened, so it made it look like the giant cat at the top would close one eye over and over, like it was dropping you a wink. It had a great big, sneaky sort of smile, too, like the Cheshire Cat in *Alice in Wonderland,* and beneath it on a billboard, it promised not only *Plenty of Girls!* but that they'd also be *Live in the Nude!*

It had been a slow night, the sleepy kind where only a few customers trickled through the door. The seats lining the runway stage were all vacant, and beyond the perimeter of the overhead spotlights and flashing strobes, it had been a veritable ghost town.

Bored and buzzing because she'd just snorted a couple bumps of coke, Elizabeth had picked "It's the End of the World as We Know It" by REM for her first stage appearance of the night. The deejay, Vinnie, had tried to talk her out of it because, as he put it: "That song's old as fuck, baby. And it ain't exactly sexy."

She'd pouted and he'd caved, and in the midst of a high-stepping march down the length of the stage to the frenetic beat, she caught sight of him: a well-dressed man with dark hair and a bemused sort of smile, standing at the end of the catwalk with a crisp one-hundred dollar bill in his hand. For a second, in the glare, he seemed surrounded by a thick shroud of shadows, an outline of impregnable darkness that made him appear taller than he really was, broader through the shoulders. She thought she saw a pair of red glowing eyes piercing out of the shadows above him, spearing into her, then the offending spotlight swung away, pivoting to another point on the stage, and the illusion abruptly ended.

"What's your name?" the man asked as she squatted, letting him slide the money beneath her G-string just above the crest of her hip.

"Fancy," she replied.

"What the hell kind of name is that?"

"The one my mama gave me," she replied with a wink. As she started to rise, he caught her by the wrist.

"Come and have a drink with me," he said. Not an invitation, but a command, like he was accustomed to saying shit exactly in this fashion and getting what he wanted every single time.

"I can't," she replied, yanking loose. "I'm dancing right now."

"When you're finished, then," he said, probably the closest he'd get to ever saying *please*.

Elizabeth rolled her eyes. "We'll see."

Of course, when she was through, she joined him at his table. After all, she wasn't fucking stupid. He'd given her a Benjamin on a night when she'd otherwise have been lucky to walk home with twenty bucks in her pocket. He ordered a Jack Daniels and Diet Coke for her, and a gin and tonic for himself, and between the two of them, they knocked back three or four apiece over the course of the next few hours. Periodically, he'd offer up another of those pristine C-notes, so she'd scoot her chair back and dance some more, up close and personal.

"What time do you get off?" he asked after she'd collected the third such tip, nipping it from his hand with her teeth while she reached behind her to refasten her sequined bikini top.

"Why?" she asked.

"I want to buy you breakfast."

"Oh," she said with a disappointed pout as she tucked the money into her waistband. "I was hoping you'd want to fuck."

And that, as the saying goes, was that. They'd fallen in love, if not head over heels, then with her heels over his shoulders at least, in the front passenger seat of his aforementioned luxury car.

◆

Her mother really had named her Fancy, just like in an old Reba McIntire song most people had never even heard anymore. Said so right on her birth certificate, right above the empty space where her father's name should have been but was conspicuously vacant.

"Of course, I know who it is," she'd told Elizabeth more than once, but she'd died from an overdose when Elizabeth had been twelve without ever sharing that particular little tidbit of information. Not that it mattered, Elizabeth supposed.

After having sex with Robert on the night they met, she let him take her to the Waffle House two blocks down and they sat facing each other in a dingy booth with a sticky tabletop between them while he nursed a cup of coffee, and she tore up a plateful of pork chops and eggs.

"What's your real name?" he asked.

"Fancy Elizabeth Mulroney," she replied around a mouthful of hashbrowns served scattered, smothered, and covered. "What's yours?"

"Robert," he told her. "Robert Landon Mapother."

It was a dignified sounding name, one that smacked of money, even if the Bentley in the parking lot hadn't already given that much away. As it turns out, Robert Mapother's father and older brother were both some hot-shit, big-time lawyers in nearby D.C. Even though Robert hadn't followed in those footsteps—or any other discernable ones, besides—to Elizabeth, who'd grown up little more than poor white trash, that kind of wealth sounded like the closest thing to heaven she was likely to ever find.

"You want to get married, Fancy Elizabeth Mulroney?" he asked beneath the buzzing OPEN sign in the window of Waffle House. It wasn't exactly romantic, but then again, she wasn't fucking stupid.

"Sure," she replied, hitching her shoulder in a shrug. "What the hell."

◆

"Her real name is Fancy. Can you believe it?"

Elizabeth hated Robert's family from the first time they ever met, but none of them more than his sister-in-law, Vanessa. Beautiful, tall, long-legged and lean, Vanessa had likely never worried about anything more bothersome than what she should wear to any of her elegant, endless parade of social engagements and charitable events. With dark hair, high cheek bones and the perfect amount of filler for just the perfect pout, Vanessa was elegantly, effortlessly beautiful, and from the moment of their introduction, she looked down her perfectly sculpted, oh-so-slightly upturned nose at Elizabeth with undisguised contempt.

"Fancy," she said again with a scoff, speaking to another woman in the bathroom at Elizabeth's wedding reception. Although posh, the celebration was relatively private and small, as had been the ceremony itself. The Mapothers were "old money," as the saying went, and years earlier, Vanessa's wedding to Robert's brother, Matthew, had boasted well over 300 guests from different political, business, and entertainment backgrounds. None of them had turned up for Robert's nuptials, however, and Elizabeth couldn't fight the suspicion that the entire thing had been kept low key for a reason.

"I think we had a cat named that once," Vanessa continued, and the other woman laughed. They'd entered the bathroom shortly behind Elizabeth, but she had the stall door closed between them, so they didn't realize she was there.

"You know why he married her, don't you?" Vanessa asked the other woman, and Elizabeth found herself now pressed against the door, breath baited as she listened.

"He's laughing at us," Vanessa said. "All this time, we've told him to choose, and he kept putting us off, making excuses, delaying the inevitable. And now this! It's all a big joke to him. That girl must be the most ridiculous, trashy thing he could find…"

In the bathroom stall, her cheeks blazing with shame and outrage, Elizabeth listened as their high-heeled soles clicked and clacked against the floor. With a soft rush, the bathroom door swung open, then shut again, and Vanessa's voice faded as they walked away.

◆

"Do you love me?" Elizabeth asked Robert once they'd arrived at their honeymoon suite. They were supposed to leave first thing in the morning for a two week-stay in the Bahamas, and while she should have still been tipsy from champagne, buzzing off both the excitement of the day and the anticipation of their honeymoon, instead, she kept replaying Vanessa's words in her mind, growing more and more pissed each time.

You know why he married her, don't you? It's all a big joke. That girl must be the most ridiculous, trashy thing he could find.

Robert, who'd been drunk for the better part of the reception, tossed his tuxedo jacket onto the floor and wrestled with his tie. "It's a little late to be asking that now, don't you think?" he said with a laugh. He gave her a lopsided, hungry look. "Get out of that dress already. I want to fuck."

In response, Elizabeth folded her arms across her chest. "Why did your family try to hide our wedding?"

"What are you talking about? They were right there, Matthew and Vanessa both. Hardly hiding, if you ask me." He snickered. "It's not like they were going to dig my folks up out of the ground for the occasion. I mean, no offense, but..." He glanced around as if readying to drop a secret on her, then added, "That would've killed the mood."

She ignored his attempts at humor. "I saw pictures of Matthew and Vanessa's wedding online. They got married at the National Cathedral, for Christ's sake. Meanwhile, ours was where…? Out in the middle of nowhere."

He laughed again. "It was at the headquarters for the Corvus Society, one of the oldest, most prestigious and exclusive civic organizations in the United States."

"Yeah? And how many people get married there each year?" she demanded, then thrust out her hands, cupping them together to form an O. "A big fat *none* besides us! Why is that, do you think? Why the fuck is that?"

It finally seemed to dawn on him that she wasn't playing around, that she was, in fact, actually pissed. His lopsided smile flatlined, and for a split second, she felt bad, because he looked like a little kid who'd gotten pushed down into a mud puddle and laughed at by his schoolmates.

Then she remembered what Vanessa had said, and any sympathy she felt abruptly died.

"Your family hates me," she said, and when he tried to protest, she shouted at him: "They think I'm a joke, and you knew they would. That's why you asked me to marry you in the first place. You don't love me at all, do you? You just wanted to mess with them. And ha, ha, ha, what better way to do that than to hook up with a stripper, right? Right?"

She couldn't believe how close she hovered to tears. Nothing ever made her cry, goddamn it, because she'd been through enough, seen enough to know there wasn't much out there except for disappointment and struggle. She knew all of that—had known all along, goddamn it—but even so, things with Robert had felt like a dream come true, a veritable fairy tale ending to the shit-show saga that had been her life up to that point, enough so that she'd even started to imagine she might be in love.

She started to storm past him, meaning to lock herself in the bathroom because she'd be damned if he'd see her cry. He caught her by the crook of the elbow, and just as she moved to tear herself away, to scream at him again, she saw his face, the profound and inexplicable sorrow in his eyes and stopped.

"That's not why I married you," he said.

She jerked her arm loose. "Then why did you?"

"Because the first time I saw you, you had this huge, shit-eating grin on your face, and you were dancing your heart out like the club wasn't empty and people weren't paying any attention to you. You didn't give a shit and you just kept on dancing." His eyes glinted as they welled with tears. "I told myself 'that's the girl I'm going to marry.' And I meant it."

How could she stay angry with him after saying something like that? Torn with indecision, Elizabeth glanced between him and the bathroom door. "Goddamn it, Robert…"

"You were right," he told her. "There's always a catch."

She didn't understand. Not even a little. "What are you talking about?"

The corners of his mouth lifted in a forlorn sort of smile. "I'll show you."

He opened his suitcase and rifled around inside, producing a strange case, one that looked like old, weatherbeaten leather, but he said was made from human skin.

"What?" she exclaimed, recoiling as he offered it to her. "That's nasty! Whose?"

"The first one like me," Robert said, and he pointed to something on the outside of the case, what looked like the sinewy red threads of an old scar: a vertical line framed by opposing triangles. He turned around and tugged his shirt tails loose from the waistband of his slacks, lifting them to reveal an identical mark just to the left of the base of his spine.

"What is that?" Elizabeth whispered, because all at once, it didn't feel like this was a joke, just a line of bullshit he was tossing out. "Did someone…do that to you? Who?"

"The man who came before me," he explained. "It's a special kind of mark, one that means you've been chosen. He used this to do it."

He thumbed open the well-worn brass latches on the case and turned back the lid. Over his shoulder, she saw the inside lined with crimson velvet. Resting against this cushioning was a long, narrow knife. The hilt appeared crafted from bronze that had dulled and darkened with age, molded in the shape of a bird with its wings outstretched, bright red gemstones, either rubies or garnets, set in the hollow sockets of its eyes.

At the sight of it, Elizabeth drew back, her puzzlement giving way to alarm, the first inklings of fear.

All at once, it occurred to her she didn't really know her new husband at all, and if marrying her had only been a joke — despite his protests to the contrary — then maybe it was high time she started to wonder — and worry — what he meant to do once the joke was up.

"I'm not supposed to have this," Robert said with a nervous laugh. "If they find out I took it, there'll be hell for me to pay, I bet."

"Who?" Elizabeth asked, retreating another step from the bed.

"My brother," he said, curling his fingers around the knife hilt with a reverent sort of care. Lamplight flashed off the slender blade as he drew it from the case. "And the Corvus Society."

It didn't make any sense to her. Had he stolen the blade from that stuffy old clubhouse where they'd gotten married? Why would Matthew give a shit if he had?

"R-Robert," she said, her voice shaking. "Listen, I'm sorry I said those things. I'm sorry I yelled. Let's just forget the whole thing, yeah?" She tried to laugh but it came out nervous and shrill. "I…I'm just going to take my bag and go. I won't say anything, I swear to God. Not a single—"

"Please don't," he whispered without looking at her. "You don't have to be afraid. I'm not going to hurt you."

"Then…then what…?" she hiccupped, staring not at him but the knife.

He turned to her. "That's not why I brought this tonight. I just…I wanted to tell you the truth. All of it. And I wanted you to see it, so you'd know. So you'd believe me."

"About what?"

"The mark on my back," he told her. "The man who had it before me was my uncle. I was thirteen when his turn was up, when he..." His voice faltered and brows lifted, his expression pleading, the face of that pitiful, lonely little boy again.

"It's my turn," he whispered. "I only have seventeen years left."

◆

"They kept him alive as long as they could," Robert said. They'd moved to the bed now and sat side by side, each of them smoking a cigarette and using one of the complimentary coffee cups as an ashtray between them.

"My uncle Eric had been involved in a car accident," he continued. "He used to do Formula One racing, as I understand, traveling all over the world to compete. He was in California, had one of his Porsches out for a run. The car went out of control, smashed into a light pole. The woman he was with, his wife, died instantly. He was legally brain dead, but they kept him hooked up to ventilators and dialysis machines."

"How horrible," Elizabeth whispered.

"I hadn't seen him in years," Robert said, twisting slightly to point to the scars on his back. "Not since he'd done this to me when I was a kid. After his accident, they kept him down in the basement of the Corvus Society's headquarters."

Startled, she drew back. "You mean...where we got married?"

He nodded. "It was years after the accident, more than a decade at least, before I saw him again. My father took me down there. Eric looked like a husk…like a mummy or something, all shriveled up and twisted, with tubes running in and out of him, all these machines beeping and whirring." With a slight shudder, he added, "I'll never forget those fucking sounds."

"Why?" she asked. "Why would your family keep him like that?"

"Because they had to," he said grimly. "There was no other choice. Whatever it took to get thirty years out of him."

"What?"

"I told you, remember? All the money in the world, anything you could ever want. But only for thirty years."

"But…" she said. "But that…that was just…"

A joke, she meant to say, because that was all it had been, hadn't it? A hypothetical game the two of them had played. Nothing serious or real.

"They kept Eric alive until his thirty years were up. Then it became my turn."

"You keep saying that," she said with a frown. "I don't understand. Your turn for what? Your family's loaded. They can't just cut you in and out of the money. There are laws and shit against that, you know."

She wasn't sure on that point, but surely to God there were. Even rich people had to play by the rules, at least sometimes, didn't they?

"My family made a deal a long, long time ago," Robert told her. With a snicker, he took a drag off his smoke.

"That's how they got so rich. They sold their souls, I guess you could say. Or at least, they sold mine."

"You mean, to the devil?" Her frown deepened. "You're saying your family's a bunch of devil worshippers?"

"It's not the devil," he said. "Not like in the Bible or anything like that. And no, they don't worship it. They tricked it. It's as stuck in this arrangement as my uncle Eric was—and me." Another snort of laughter. "I'd feel sorry for the son of a bitch, except eventually it's going to kill me."

He's not kidding, she realized, wide-eyed and stunned. What he was saying couldn't possibly be real, sounded like complete and absolute bullshit, but somehow, even so, she could see it in his eyes. His resignation and fear. His anger.

"I have seventeen years left until that happens," he told her with a wan sort of smile.

"And then…you die," she said. "This devil-thing, it comes up from Hell, and…what? Rips you apart or something?" Her mind spun with all the shitty horror movies she'd ever seen. "Swallows your soul?"

"It's a demon, actually," Robert corrected, snubbing his cigarette out against the inside of the cup. "And for the record, it's not down in Hell." He turned to her with a thin smile devoid of anything resembling humor. "It's in me."

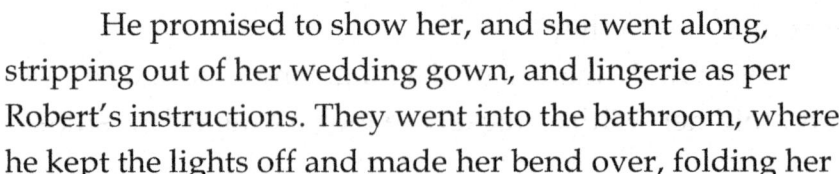

He promised to show her, and she went along, stripping out of her wedding gown, and lingerie as per Robert's instructions. They went into the bathroom, where he kept the lights off and made her bend over, folding her arms against the smooth, cold stone of the sink counter and resting her head in the nest of her elbows.

This is bullshit, she thought as the flat muscles of his groin slapped repeatedly, rhythmically against her ass, and why he thought he had to play these weird games with her — on their wedding night, for fuck's sake — after they'd spent the last few weeks going at it like rabbits without pretense was beyond her.

Then she looked up and saw her reflection in the mirror, and instead of Robert fucking her from behind, she saw someone else altogether — some*thing* dark and looming that seemed to fill the entire bathroom, and tower over her, its head nearly flush with the ceiling. Although she couldn't make out anything clearly in its form, its eyes blazed above her, bright red and alight, like embers or coals in a fireplace. When their gazes met, it threw its massive head back and roared, the walls and ceiling shuddering around them, the mirror rattling in its frame. She saw it had wings — spreading now as it arched its spine — and as she opened her mouth and began to shriek, it occurred to her dimly that the creature was at once both the most beautiful and terrifying apparition she'd ever beheld.

Two years later, as she finished getting ready for a black-tie engagement, Elizabeth caught part of a segment on the local evening news.

"...police are still searching for any leads into the disappearance early Saturday morning of thirteen-year-old Josh Finley," the anchor was saying.

Elizabeth had her back to the screen as she finished putting in her earring but turned now as a picture flashed into view: a middle-school yearbook shot of a boy with sandy hair and a broad, beaming smile.

"...the eighth-grader from Wyman Park disappeared within a few blocks of his home, leaving only his bicycle abandoned on the side of the road—" the newscaster continued, cutting short as Robert turned the TV off.

"He's the one, then?" Elizabeth asked. "Josh Finley? I like him. He's pretty."

"Who cares?" Robert made a melodramatic point of pushing the cuff of his tuxedo jacket back and checking his watch. "We're not keeping him anyway."

Surprised, she turned to him. "But I thought we had to?"

"The only thing we *have* to do is keep the little shit alive for the next fifteen years," Robert said. "I figure Traynor can do as good a job of that as anybody."

But he's a perv, she thought of saying. A genuine, Grade-A pedophile. Michael Traynor, who'd abducted Josh Finley, had already tried hocking them another kid only a month or two earlier, pale and scrawny, with dirty blond hair and haunted eyes that Robert had shelled out over fifteen thousand dollars to buy. She imagined he was still licking his wounds over that one, having his personal preference vetoed. This was his way of sulking because he didn't get his way. For a man fast approaching thirty years old, Robert could be such a baby sometimes.

"I guess," she said, rolling her eyes again. Poor little guy, she thought, because Josh Finley really would be a looker someday. In the meantime, he was in for some hard knocks.

Literally, thanks to Traynor, she thought with a snicker.

"Are you ready yet?" Robert asked, any pretense of patience gone. When he glowered at her, she saw his eyes had turned black, anything discernable of his corneas or irises lost behind that sudden, glinting, obsidian veil. His shadow seemed to loom behind him, impossibly huge, ridiculously wide, the sides stretching out like smoky wings unfurling.

He could pull that shit all he wanted. She wasn't scared of him—or what was inside him.

"Just let me grab my mask, darling," she said. She only ever called him this when he encroached upon her last damn nerve, which seemed lately to be with ever-growing frequency.

She lifted it carefully from her dressing table: heavy panels of thick leather that had been painted gold at her specific request, festooned with sequins to match her Carolina Herrera gown for the evening. Robert had one, too, a replica of a medieval plague doctor's mask, except his had been dyed red. Everyone else in the Corvus Society would have black masks to wear, including Matthew and the ever-insufferable Vanessa. After all, it was a very special occasion they would be celebrating: the selection at long last of Robert's successor.

As she settled her mask into place, she turned in a semi-circle, the long skirt of her gown fanning out beneath her. "How do I look?"

Robert glanced at his watch again rather than his wife. "The car's been waiting downstairs. Let's go."

With that, he turned on his heel and strode smartly for the door.

Fifteen more years, she thought. She could put up with Robert that long, right? For all the money in the world?

Lowering her mask, Elizabeth screwed her face up and flipped him off. "Coming, darling," she crooned.

After all, she wasn't fucking stupid.

This story is continued in the novel THE VESSEL, available in ebook and paperback from Wicked House Publishing.

What Fresh Hell Is This?

"It's nice to see you again, Dr. Cooper," the man said before Shannon even had the chance to greet him, never mind introduce herself. Caught off-guard by his unexpected familiarity, she closed the door to the small interrogation room and frowned.

"I'm sorry. Have we met?"

The man cracked an almost rueful smile. "Before today? No."

Bryce must have told him who I was. As she thought this, Shannon glanced at the video camera in the corner by the ceiling. She knew Detective Bryce Haynes and other police investigators were on the other side of that glinting lens, watching every move she and the suspect made, listening to their every word.

"Mr. Paulson, I'm a forensic psychiatrist," she told the man, looking down at the file in her hand. "I work with law enforcement and the courts."

Arthur Alan Paulson, his case face sheet read, followed by his date of birth, home address, height, and weight, along with his booking number and the charges filed against him: *Aggravated Murder – Premeditated,* and *Felonious Assault – Victim Seriously Harmed.*

"Can you tell me what the date is today?" Shannon asked.

"October fifteenth." Paulson sat with his hands folded on top of the table in an almost prayer-like posture, his wrists cuffed together by a short length of gleaming silver chain.

"Do you know who the President of the United States is?"

He chuckled. "Yes, unfortunately."

She awarded him a disapproving frown as she slid the chair back across from him and sat. "These questions may seem silly, but they're important to determine your mental orientation. I'd like you to answer to the best of your ability. Now, can you tell me where you are?"

His smile grew strained. "I have no idea."

"You're in the Cooke County jail," she told him. "And I'd like to speak with you about what happened earlier today, the events that brought you here. Would that be alright?"

"Do I really have much of a choice?" he asked.

"There's always a choice, Mr. Paulson," she replied. "Before we get started, I have to advise you that even though I'm a psychiatrist, this conversation won't fall under the traditional doctor-patient confidentiality rules. What we talk about, what if anything you choose to share with me, will be a matter of record, and potentially used against you in a court of law. As such, you're entitled to have an attorney present—"

"No, thanks."

"Are you sure? Again, I have to let you know that anything you say—"

"—can be used against me. I understand."

Shannon cut her gaze at the camera again, then back to the suspect. He hadn't asked for an attorney even once since being arrested. Bryce and the other detectives were chomping at the bit to interrogate him, but cooler heads had ultimately prevailed, and Shannon had been called in first. Her job was simple: assess Paulson's current mental status and determine whether he was of sound enough mind to undergo police questioning.

Leaning forward, she placed a digital recorder on the table between them. "I'm going to record our conversation," she said, and he nodded. "Let's start with you telling me a little about yourself."

She usually had to prod patients more, dance around with questions that began generally enough, but eventually narrowed down to more pointed and pertinent specifics, but as if realizing her angle, understanding what she was looking for without her having to dig, Paulson answered easily, describing a normal enough childhood in an upper-middle-class Roman Catholic family. He'd married his college sweetheart, he told Shannon, and together, they shared three children, two cats, and a modest split-level ranch in the suburbs just outside town. He held a degree in accounting and had worked for more than fifteen years for Belflower and Howell, one of the world's largest financial corporations. He was a mid-level manager with good performance reviews and a tenured track toward a comfortable retirement by the time he turned sixty-five.

That is, until that morning, when he'd arrived at Belflower and Howell with a KelTec PMR-30 semi-automatic pistol loaded with a 30-round, high-capacity magazine.

What happened? she wondered, although for the time being, she kept this question to herself. Why did a middle-aged man of such an ordinary background suddenly snap in such a violent way? As he spoke, Paulson struck her as a completely calm, rational, and—dare she say it?—*sane* individual.

"Were your parents ever abusive toward you?" she asked.

"They used to spank me for acting up, and my dad would use his belt sometimes, but nothing I'd consider real abuse."

Shannon inclined her head. "You don't consider being hit with a belt abusive?"

"It was the way things were done back then," he said. "When we were bad, we took the licks we had coming. Plain and simple."

"Your coworkers," she said, treading lightly. "Did you feel they had licks coming, then? They were bad?"

Eighteen people were dead, and seven others wounded, tying the mass shooting at Belflower and Howell for tenth place on the list of most deadly in U.S. history.

As if understanding the gravity of this grim distinction, Paulson regarded her for a long moment, then said, "Don't you think if I could take it back somehow and change things, I would? God knows I've tried."

"What do you mean?"

He opened his mouth as if to answer, then seemed to think better of it. "Never mind."

Shannon turned through the pages in her file folder. "Mr. Paulson, you were recently passed over for a promotion within the Financial Planning and Analysis department where you worked, am I right?"

His shoulders sagged with unhappy resignation. "Yes."

"The man who received that promotion, Eric Gorman, had been a subordinate on your team, someone you'd helped train?"

"Yes."

"He was younger than you. Correct?" she asked, and when he didn't answer, she continued. "In fact, Eric Gorman was born the same year as your daughter, Clarice, which makes him young enough to be your son. But with that promotion, he would have become your immediate supervisor, your boss. Were you disappointed about that? Frustrated, even angry?"

Paulson had killed Gorman first that morning, walking into the other man's office and plugging a .22 Magnum round through his head. The shot obliterated Gorman's face in a mess of shattered bone and mangled meat, redecorating the back wall with blood and splattered brain matter.

"The police saw where Edith filed for divorce last month," Shannon said. "She cited irreconcilable differences as the grounds. That ranch house you mentioned, you don't live there anymore. You moved out and found your own apartment, right? That would have been around the time the news about Eric's promotion hit, too. Those are enormous stressors, back to back for you."

"We'd been talking about it for a while," he mumbled, studying his hands. "Edi and me, we've both known the divorce has been a long time coming."

"Still, it must hurt."

"We tried to make it work." Lifting his head, he looked up at her, his smile ragged. "Went to counseling at church and everything. They keep telling us divorce is a sin, but Edi doesn't see another way. 'I want out, Art.' That's what she said."

She didn't miss the way his expression shifted, his lips drawing down when he said the word *church*. "You're Catholic, you said?"

"Born and raised, lifelong. But the way the priest made it sound, the whole place would've burned to the ground, struck by lightning, if I walked back in after getting divorced." His grimace deepened. "Like I haven't tithed my ten percent every week for the past twenty-five years."

"How did that make you feel?"

"How the hell do you think?" he snapped, his voice sharp enough to startle. Seeming to compose himself immediately, he drew in a deep breath, then tried again. "It made me furious, of course."

"At the church? Your wife? Belflower and Howell?"

"Take your pick," he said with another low sigh, the shadows falling heavily into the lines and hollows of his face. "I had thirteen years left until I was set to retire. I told Edi, let's just make it until then, and we can move down to Cocoa Beach or wherever the hell she'd like, and start all over. Build something new. But she couldn't wait—she *wouldn't.* She'd had enough, she said, because I worked too much, only to hear them tell of it at Belflower and Howell, I didn't work *enough,* at least not to get that promotion."

Shannon watched him wordlessly, the way the bright glare from the overhead fluorescent fixture shined against the greasy sheen on the balding crown of his head. His thin hair lay slicked-down and combed over in a failed attempt to cover that pale, exposed dome of flesh. The collar of his shirt lay open because they'd made him take his tie off during processing, along with his belt and shoestrings.

"Just in case he tries to pull an Epstein," Bryce had told her, tilting his head at an awkward angle and holding his fist above him, miming a hanging.

Bryce had met her at the front entrance upon her arrival, putting his arm around her and ushering her past the crowd of reporters. The jail had been an absolute madhouse, the street outside logjammed with news vans in either direction, the sidewalk overflowing with camera crews, the air humming with the drone of helicopters circling overhead.

"We got word from the hospital a little while ago," Bryce had told her as they made their way inside. "One of the victims who'd been in critical condition passed away earlier. That brings us up to eighteen now, with at least another handful still hit-or-miss on surviving the night."

She'd braced herself to meet a monster in that interrogation room, but instead, Arthur Paulson looked old, weary, and weatherbeaten to her, and even though he'd done something horrific less than twelve hours earlier, she wasn't jaded or cynical enough yet in her clinical role to not feel a twinge of pity for him.

"May I ask you something, Dr. Cooper?" Paulson asked, and again, it struck her as odd, how he knew her name, how it rolled off his tongue like they were old acquaintances, if not friends.

"Of course," she replied.

"Do you believe in God?"

"Yes, I do."

Not devoutly or anything, and she hadn't stepped foot in a church in over a decade except to be a bridesmaid in one friend or another's wedding. She wasn't one to pray, not even for the stupid little things that people often prayed for, like good luck, or the winning lottery number, or to make it a handful of blocks to the nearest gas station when their car was running on fumes. Still, she supposed she believed in a higher power, if not the Christian God, per se, then a being of some omnipotence.

Is that part of the reason he did this? she wondered. *Some sort of God complex? Feeling powerless to control the events in his life, he seized something he could: letting people live or die.*

"Tell me," Paulson said. "What do you think happens when we die?"

He was inviting her along a slippery slope. Those with a God complex believed themselves to be above reproach or common laws. Associated with the clinical diagnosis of Narcissistic Personality Disorder, it was part of a series of self-defense mechanisms to combat feelings of inferiority. Dismissing or rebuking this turn in conversation could potentially blow any chance she may have of building rapport with him, but giving into it, playing along, could reinforce or further fuel his delusions.

Shannon chose her response carefully. "The Bible says people who are good go to Heaven."

"And those who aren't...?"

"They go to Hell."

"And do you believe that?"

She studied him for a moment. "Eighteen people died today by your hand. Regardless of what awaits in the afterlife, you're going to have to face the consequences of your actions here on earth."

"I agree," he said. "One hundred percent, wholeheartedly. I'm sorry for what happened, for what I did. And like I've told you before, if I could take it back, change it, then I would. I've tried, over and over, but it makes no difference."

"I don't understand. What do you mean, you've tried to change it?"

His eyes glimmered with a helpless light, tears welling. "I mean I've tried throwing the gun off the bridge into the river. I've slashed my own tires so I can't leave the house, even called Eric personally and begged him not to come to work today. I've tried to kill myself a thousand different ways—gunshot, hanging, wrist-cutting, pills. I've done everything I could—anything I could think of—to try and make this horrible day stop, but it...*it just keeps happening!*"

With a ragged cry, he clapped his hands to his face, his fingers hooked like claws into his brows.

Bewildered, Shannon blinked at him, then at the camera again. She could almost feel Bryce meeting her gaze through the lens, his expression as baffled as she knew hers must be.

"I don't understand," she said again. "What do you mean?"

Paulson lowered his hands, his face splotchy and flushed. "Today's like a record stuck on repeat, replaying the same song. No matter what I do, it starts all over, again and again. I can't take it anymore. I just can't!"

Leaning across the table, he caught her by the hands, so quickly and desperately, he knocked her folder to the floor, scattering the contents.

"Help me," he pleaded. "For God's sake, make it stop!"

◆

"You're not going back in there," Bryce told her.

No sooner had Paulson grabbed her than the door to the interrogation room burst open, with Bryce and several uniformed officers rushing in to the rescue. Only, as Shannon continued to insist as they stood facing each other in the corridor, she hadn't needed or wanted any.

"Yes, I am," she said, giving her arm a jerk to free herself from his grasp. "I haven't finished my assessment, which means if you question him, anything he tells you is likely to be tossed out as inadmissible in court."

"Then I'm going in with you," Bryce insisted, and she hated his bullshit macho routine, like she was either an imbecile or a child, because she was neither.

This is exactly what I've been afraid of all along, she wanted to tell him, but held her tongue, even though by now, anyone with half a brain and a working set of eyeballs in the homicide division had likely figured out they were sleeping together. *You getting hung up on me, not keeping this casual, noncommittal.*

"If you go back in that interrogation room with me, any rapport I've managed to build with Paulson so far—which isn't much, trust me—may as well be wadded up and tossed in the trash. Then he'll either clam up, lawyer up, or both, and that'll put us right back where we started."

Paulson hadn't attacked her, she told Bryce, despite his insistence to the contrary. He hadn't been trying to hurt her, but rather, when he grabbed her, to Shannon it had felt like the desperate efforts of a man hanging onto the crumbling edge of a very steep precipice, one that threatened to break apart beneath his fingertips and send him tumbling to his death.

"Let me do my job," she told Bryce as she brushed past him, heading back for the interrogation room, all-too aware of the side glances and thinly veiled attention they'd drawn from other cops in the corridor. Yep, she realized glumly. *So much for keeping things on the down low.*

• • ———————◆——————— • •

"I'm sorry," Paulson said, shamefaced and sheepish as she resumed her seat at the table across from him. "I didn't mean to hurt you."

"You didn't," Shannon reassured. "When you reached for me, it startled me, that's all. And the police officers, too. But everything's okay now, and we can get back to our conversation. I'd like to pick up where we left off. You told me today is like a record stuck on repeat. Can you tell me why?"

He hesitated, as if reluctant now to admit this. "You'll think I'm crazy."

"I don't like to use that word," Shannon said, and when this coaxed him to lift his gaze, she smiled at him gently. "What did you mean?"

After a moment, again as if debating whether or not to answer, he said, "Do you remember this old movie? It had Bill Murray in it. He kept living the same day over and over. Every time he woke up, he found himself back where he started, and the events of the day would play out almost exactly as they had before, no matter what he did to try and change them."

She'd heard of the movie, of course: *Groundhog Day.*

"Do you think that's what's happening to you?" she asked. "You're reliving the same day over and over?"

"Yes," he said quietly, no more than a whisper. His eyes were round and shadow-rimmed, his appearance haggard and haunted.

"Why do you think that?"

"Because it's true. I wake up every morning and it's October fifteenth. Over and over again."

"How do you know?"

"I see it on my phone," he said. "On the television, the internet. I see the same news headlines every single morning, hear the same songs on the radio, see the exact same people in the exact same clothes, doing and saying the exact same things, over and over and over."

"But we all see the same people every day," Shannon said. "Many of them, anyway. It's easy to think someone's wearing the same clothes, if they wear similar styles or colors more than once in a given week. Do you think that—"

"I see the date on my phone," he said again, more sharply this time. "On the TV, I told you, on my computer screen at work! October fifteenth, all day, every day! I've lost count of how many times I've lived through it."

There was no point in arguing with him, she knew, so instead, she switched tacks. "What would your estimate be?"

"I...I don't know. A hundred times, maybe? A thousand?"

"And you said you've taken steps to try and stop what happened. Do you mean the shooting? You've tried committing suicide to prevent it, you said, sabotaging your car, calling your boss at home."

He nodded at each. "Yes."

"What happened when you did those things?"

"When I try to kill myself? I wake up right away, right back where I started, October fifteenth all over again. Even when I cut my tires, I still found myself somehow arriving at the office. Something always happened and I was there. Even if I tried to throw the gun away, it would wind up back in my hand again."

"Do you think you're exaggerating?" she asked. "That you're wrong? What you're describing to me isn't possible, Mr. Paulson."

"I know how it sounds, but it's the truth. I'm not lying, or exaggerating. It's real, it's happening to me." He stared at her, desperate and pleading, then his shoulders slumped. "Never mind. You're not going to believe me this time. No matter what I say."

"This time?" she repeated. "Have I believed you before, then?"

"Not often. But a few times, yeah. Enough so that I keep trying." He added this last with a bitter laugh.

"So, we meet each time? Whenever the day repeats, and the shooting recurs, you and I sit together and talk like this?"

"Usually yes. Sometimes it's in a hospital, if they bring me there first. Sometimes you visit in my jail cell."

"You know what you're saying is impossible, right?" she said again. "It defies the laws of physics and time. Yet, you say it's happening. How do you explain that?"

"I thought at first, it was because I had the chance to do things over again, make it right somehow. You know, like in that movie? But like I said before, I've tried. God knows I have, but it hasn't made any difference. Not in the end. They all still end up dead because of me. I even tried going to confession, begging God for forgiveness. Still didn't do any good."

"What do you think that means? That God has forsaken you?"

"Maybe I thought that at first. But not anymore. I don't think He's forsaken me; I think He's *judged* me. Like you said before, good people go to Heaven when they die. Bad people..."

His voice faltered with a shallow gulp.

"...go to Hell," she finished for him. "Is that what you think has happened? Where you think you are?"

Paulson looked at her, his eyes glassy but still remarkably sane. "Yes. I think this is Hell."

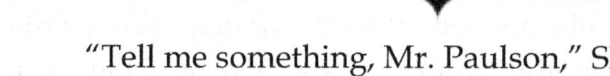

"Tell me something, Mr. Paulson," Shannon said. They'd taken another short break in the interview, this time so she could get them each something to drink — a diet soda for herself, and bottled water for him — and have a chance to process what he'd shared. "Why do you think you're in Hell?"

"Because of what I did. I shot Eric and the others. I did a terrible thing, and there's no undoing it. I deserve to be punished."

She knew Bryce would be ecstatic in the other room about the admission, especially since she wasn't there to remind him it didn't mean jack shit if in the same measure of breath, Paulson expressed persecutory delusions.

"Let's unpack this, then," she said to Paulson. "You believe you committed a sin, a terrible series of them, for which God has decided you should be punished, correct? He's sent you to Hell. But God doesn't do that, doesn't judge people for their sins until after they've died. How could He have judged you, then?"

"I must have died. Maybe I shot myself after…what happened. Or maybe the police…?"

"You don't know?"

"It changes every day. I told you, I try to stop the shootings, but they just keep happening. It's happened so much, I can't keep track of it in my head anymore, where one version of today stops and another begins, what happened the first time around, what didn't."

"But as far as you know, as much as you remember, you didn't die. In this 'version' of today, at least. Would that be fair to say? Right now, you're awake, alive, and talking to me."

He looked uncertain but conceded with a nod.

"And I'm awake, alive, and talking with you, too," she said. "Which begs another question, then. If you're in Hell, reliving this day over and over, where does that leave the rest of us? All the people you've interacted with and seen today, wouldn't that mean we're all stuck in the same time loop right along with you? How could none of us realize that, the same way you did?"

"I don't know. Maybe it's because this is my punishment. My own private Hell." Lifting his hands, his cuffs jangling, he covered his face. "Maybe that's it. None of you are real. No one is except me."

"But earlier, you reached out, Mr. Paulson. You touched me, grabbed my hands. How do you explain that, if I'm not real?"

"I…I don't know."

"If that's not enough, if touching me, hearing my voice, seeing me with your own eyes doesn't prove to you that I'm real—if you don't trust your senses, Mr. Paulson, then how can I prove it to you? Or rather, how can you prove to *yourself* that I'm real? What would convince you of that?"

Because maybe, she thought, if she could persuade him to admit to that fallacy, then the foundation upon which his complex delusions had been constructed would begin to crack.

He closed his eyes and tented his fingers together, again almost as if praying. "What did you have for dinner last night?"

The question stopped her short. At first, she meant to steer the conversation back on track, toward her ultimate goal of dismantling the warped logic behind his beliefs, then it occurred to her that she didn't know the answer. It was a mundane enough piece of information, it may not have immediately bobbed to the surface of her mind like a fishing float after a successful cast, but with a moment or two of thought, nonetheless, it should have come to her. But it didn't, and the harder she tried to remember, the higher that brick wall in her mind seemed to become.

What *had* she eaten? Some tasteless, reheated Lean Cuisine she'd overcooked in the microwave? An overpriced entrée from a restaurant she and Bryce had visited? Fast food tacos from a drive-through near her apartment?

Come to think of it...

As she tried to remember exactly where her apartment was—or even if she lived in one, instead of a house—she found she couldn't. All at once, a million things that should have been well-worn and familiar to her, small and simple details like her phone number, her birthday, her favorite movie, book, or song—none came to mind. She felt only a dim and distant itch inside her brain, like a word or phrase caught on the tip of her tongue, tantalizingly just beyond reach.

"Dr. Cooper?" Paulson asked, and she startled out of her troubled reverie, blinking at him.

With a weak laugh and even frailer smile, she said, "Why don't we take another short break? I'll ask one of the officers to go with you to the restroom, if you'd like."

"Don't tell me that son of a bitch got to you," Bryce said, having followed her into the break room. He leaned against a nearby counter, watching as she poured coffee from a decanter into a Styrofoam cup. When she finished, he nudged a plastic caddy toward her, offering sugar and powdered creamer packets.

"Of course not." But as she reached for the caddy, it occurred to her that she didn't know how she took her coffee, if she preferred it black, or with anything added. Not that she couldn't remember so small and simple a thing, but rather…

Like I don't know, she thought as she smacked face-first into that towering mental wall again. *Like I've never known.*

"That's good." Bryce touched her hand, a quick and fleeting gesture, and she realized she had no memory of ever having actually been with him—not a date, a kiss, making love to him, nothing. There was a vague and distant sense of familiarity within her mind toward him, a fond warmth she felt in his company, and maybe she'd mistaken this for something more—something *remembered*—all that while.

"Do you know much about Greek mythology?" she asked.

"You mean, like gods and goddesses? No, not really." Perplexed, he laughed. "Why?"

"I was just thinking, that's all. I looked something up on my phone. It's a myth about a man named Sisyphus."

"What does that have to do with anything?"

"It doesn't," she said with another weak laugh. "Not really, I'm sure. It's just…like I said, I looked it up a few minutes ago. It's about a man who's punished in the afterlife by having to push a giant boulder up the side of a mountain. It takes him all day, and right before he reaches the top, he loses his grasp and the boulder rolls back down, so he has to start over. Every day, it's exactly the same, again and again. Forever."

The word rattled in her mind, like a windchime made from hollow bits of bone.

Forever.

His punishment in Hell forever.

"Paulson's crazy, Shannon," Bryce said quietly.

Is he? she wondered, staring down at his fingers as they lay draped atop her own, realizing she had no memory of him touching her anyplace else, or at any other time before that day. Even though it felt like she *should*.

"You know I don't like that word," she told him, only she didn't think Bryce knew that at all. Not really.

"You're right. I'm sorry." With a smile, he leaned in and gave her a kiss, and although she believed in her heart he wouldn't have ordinarily done so, not right there where anyone could see and set the gossip mills whirling, she was grateful and glad he'd taken that chance.

Because I don't remember ever having kissed him before.

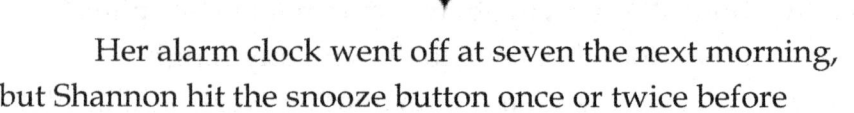

Her alarm clock went off at seven the next morning, but Shannon hit the snooze button once or twice before finally crawling out of bed in begrudging concession. She wasn't due in the office until nine, but getting up early allowed the chance to get some caffeine in her system, and a run on the treadmill in her living room before leaving for work.

As her feet pounded out a brisk rhythm, punctuated by sharp exhalations through pursed lips, Shannon watched the morning news. Many of the patients she spoke with routinely complained that the headlines anymore made them anxious or depressed, despondent even at times, and she couldn't say she blamed them, not in the uncertain and turbulent world in which they all struggled to survive.

I guess it means job security for me though, if nothing else, she thought, just as the TV cut from a segment about the ongoing war in the Middle East back to the local news desk, where a grim-faced anchor announced a breaking story.

"We've received reports that a gunman opened fire at the corporate offices of financial firm Belflower and Howell only a short time ago," he said, as in a sidebar video, aerial footage overlooking a towering building was shown. The streets surrounding it were ringed with police squad cars, red and blue lights flashing, and she could see SWAT personnel in tactical gear rushing toward the main entrance. A banner in the upper corner of the screen read: *LIVE – October 15, 8:27 A.M.*

"Portions of the building have been evacuated," the anchor continued, "with other departments being warned to shelter in place until police have secured the scene. At this time, the number of casualties is unconfirmed, but we're hearing reports of at least a dozen victims, if not more. The gunman is as yet unidentified and police have released no official word on any…"

Great, Shannon thought, knowing her phone would soon be lighting up like a Christmas tree with inbound calls and texts. It was her turn to have drawn the short stick and be on-call; if the shooter was apprehended alive, she'd be the one police would summon for a mental health assessment. At least, though, she'd get to see Bryce for a little while in the process.

Maybe later on, we could grab drinks and dinner at that one little place we both like so much, she thought, although for the life of her, she couldn't recall the name of it now, despite it being their favorite restaurant.

It will come to me eventually, she told herself as she continued to run. *These things always do.*

Just Deserts

"You've hardly touched your food," Dee lamented from the doorway. "Aren't you hungry?"

Caroline looked at the two dozen soft-shell supremes from Taco Bell littering the table drawn across her bed. It was the kind you find in hospitals—like the bed itself, where the head and foot could raise or lower with the touch of a button. The mattress was filled with sand, and jettisons of air would periodically inflate one side or the other, shifting her body from right to left, minimizing pressure in any area for too long. It was so loud Caroline would have to turn her television volume nearly full blast to hear over the din, but Dr. Consuelo said it was necessary to prevent skin breakdown.

At least until I can get up on my own, she thought, and because her mother remained in the doorway, her expression fraught with worry, she picked up one of the tacos and unwrapped it. As bits of shredded lettuce and cheese tumbled across the front of her gown, she took a bite.

"I'm fine, Mom."

Dee lingered a moment longer at the threshold, watching as Caroline chewed. "Alright, then. Call me if you need anything." Just as she started to close the door, she paused. "Do you want me to close the blinds all the way? Is that too much light?"

"No," Caroline said quickly, and she didn't miss the flash of wariness in Dee's eyes. "I...I said I'm fine."

Dee studied her for a long, suspicious moment, then left. Not until Caroline heard the click of the latch as the door closed did she let out a low sigh, swallowing the ground beef and tortilla with a relieved gulp.

It was nearly three forty-five. The bus would be coming soon. From her bed, Caroline could see the street in front of her house, the sidewalk running parallel, and the stop sign at the far corner. Every morning, she'd watch kids from the neighborhood gather there to catch the school bus. And every afternoon, she'd watch as they returned home.

Alison, CeCe, and Toby. At least, that's how Caroline knew them. She'd named them after characters from the TV show, *Pretty Little Liars*. She told herself one day she'd learn their real names, that she'd go outside and say hello.

After my surgery, she thought, looking down at what remained of the taco in her hand. She started to wad the paper up to cover it, then her stomach warbled.

By the time the orange-yellow school bus pulled to a stop outside, its accordion side door folding back as Alison, CeCe, and Toby got off, she'd eaten eleven tacos, and had just unwrapped another.

"You have big bones." That's what Dee always told her, even from a very young age. "Big bones and chunky cheeks," she'd say, pinching Caroline's face in a way she meant to be playful, yet hurt.

That was why she'd always made sure Caroline had second helpings, if not three or four, and made her clean her plate. No whining, no wasting, that was Dee's mealtime motto. When Caroline got older — and bigger — it had gotten harder for Dee's cooking to keep up with her appetite, so they'd started relying more on takeout and fast food.

"I'm going to need another mortgage," Dee teased, but it was all in fun, she'd be quick to add, because she knew that Caroline needed to eat as much as she did.

"You're a big girl, with big bones. It's for your own good."

Growing up, it would bother Caroline that Dee wouldn't let her go out to play, especially since there were other children in the neighborhood who she'd see riding their skateboards or bikes past the house.

"They'll laugh at you," Dee had warned. "Just like the kids at school, remember?"

Of course Caroline remembered. Who could forget Brian Ainsford in second grade, who'd knocked her down during recess, then laughed because she couldn't get back up. "Like a beached whale," he'd declared, and other kids had joined him laughing, and by the time Miss Livingston had reached them, poor Caroline had been reduced to humiliated, hysterical sobs.

Dee had picked her up that afternoon, made her sit outside the principal's office while she met with him and Miss Livingston behind closed doors. Caroline had still been able to hear her mother's shrill, angry voice, punctuated by Miss Livingston's quieter, futile attempts to appease. In the end, Dee had marched out of the office and snatched Caroline by the wrist, dragging her toward the exit.

"You're never going back to this horrid place," Dee had declared, and on the way home, she'd bought an entire chocolate cake. That's what Caroline had eaten for supper that night, and if memory served, she'd polished off the whole thing.

They don't understand.

Dee's words came to her now as, through the window blinds, she watched Toby pretend to tug at Alison's backpack. She slapped his hands away, but grinned as she did, and Caroline admired how long and spindly her arms seemed.

She must have small bones, she thought, because that's why Dee said she needed to eat so much: her big bones. Her body was different. She needed so much more, and if she were to suddenly stop eating, go on one of those crash diets on TV, she would probably die of some kind of metabolic or complete cardiac collapse.

Your body's meant to be that size. That's why you've always eaten so much. It's for your own good.

Lately, though, Caroline had found herself wondering if that was true. She'd seen shows about people who weighed a lot like she did, and at first it helped her feel better, knowing she wasn't alone. Then one of the programs, *My Half-Ton Life*, changed its name to *My FORMER Half-Ton Life,* and the star, Laurel, had undergone gastric bypass. And as Laurel slimmed down, enough so she could get up out of bed on her own — a previously impossible feat — it occurred to Caroline that maybe that wasn't out of reach for her, either.

Laurel had even found a boyfriend. Caroline had watched, enthralled, as Laurel's beau smiled at her on screen and said how proud he was of her for losing the weight, how beautiful he thought she was, and how much he loved her.

Maybe I could have that, too, she thought, looking out the window, watching Toby jog across the street toward his house. *Someone who thinks I'm beautiful.*

She'd see him with his dad sometimes, as he practiced driving around the block. When he got his license, he wouldn't need the school bus anymore. He could come and go as he pleased, and that made her feel sad.

I won't get to see him as much.

She found herself imagining interactions and conversations with him, even friendship. She daydreamed about walking out the front door and approaching him at the bus stop, watching him turn to her with that broad smile she'd come to adore. She wondered what her name would sound like if he said it aloud. What his laugh sounded like. What color his eyes were.

Thoughts like that left her flushed and giggling.

"Remember when Dr. Consuelo talked about surgery?" she'd asked Dee a few weeks earlier. Dee had cut the discussion short before it even had a chance to lift off.

"Stomach stapling?" she'd cried, and even though Caroline had tried to tell her they didn't do that anymore, she would have none of it. "It's even worse now. They cut out most of your stomach! Everything except a tiny pinch, and sew what's left to your intestines, so anything you eat goes straight through you and out the other end. There'd be nothing left to digest anything, so you'd die of malnutrition. Is that what you want? To lie in bed and starve to death?

Because if it is, I don't need to pay tens of thousands of dollars to make it happen. I can just stop feeding you. You could starve to death then, and I'd be left here all alone. Would that make you happy?"

Caroline had told her of course not. She'd apologized, promising she'd never bring it up again, but in the back of her mind, she'd been lying.

Dr. Consuelo comes to see me in two weeks, she thought, because her doctors had to make house calls. She couldn't walk anymore, never mind fit into a car. *I'll make up excuses, get Mom to leave the room while he's here. Then I'll tell him the truth: I want to have the surgery.*

She heard the doorbell ring, the sound distant and faint above the rush of air as her mattress shifted, tilting her away from the window. No one ever came to visit them unannounced, so it struck her as strange. After a few minutes, the door to her bedroom opened.

"You didn't eat your lunch," Dee said.

"I ate some of it," Caroline said. "Who was at the door?"

"The boy across the street. I talked to him last week about coming over to do some yardwork, mow the grass." Dee looked back over her shoulder, called down the hall. "I'll be right there."

Caroline's eyes widened in horror. "You mean, he's here?"

"Yes, in the living room. I was on my way to get him a glass of iced tea and thought I'd see if you needed anything. Why?"

"N-nothing," Caroline said. "No reason, I...I just..."

"I'm surprised you know who he is," Dee remarked. "I mean, it's not like you've ever seen him before."

Her tone sounded light enough, but there was a hardness in her gaze that left Caroline feeling like an amoeba beneath a microscope.

"He's handsome," Dee continued. "Don't you think?"

Now Caroline felt color blazing in her cheeks. "I don't know. I...I mean..."

"You don't know?" Dee said, her voice taking on that same cold edge as her gaze. "You've been watching him all this time, and never noticed?"

"I...I haven't..." Caroline sputtered in surprise.

"Don't lie to me," Dee snapped, stepping closer to the bed. "Don't you dare. I've seen you staring out that window day in and day out, hoping to get a glimpse of him."

Caroline's throat tightened, her eyes stinging with sudden tears. "Mama..."

"Do you think he'll want you, too? Is that what you think? Haven't you learned yet? Haven't I told you enough times? Look at yourself."

"Stop," Caroline whispered. "Mama, please."

"Is that why you asked about the surgery again? You think it will make him want you? He'll think you're disgusting, nothing more than a joke. And he's never, *ever* going to want you. The only thing he'll do is laugh at you, just like they did at school."

Caroline began to cry. "Stop it."

"No one will ever love you except me," Dee said. "But you don't want to believe that, so I guess I have to prove it to you." She turned to leave, and Caroline felt a swell of panic.

"Wait! Wh-what are you going to do?"

"I'm going to bring him in here and tell him you're in love with him. I'm going to tell him how you look out the window at him all day long."

"N-no!" Caroline cried. "No, Mama, please don't! I'm sorry. I won't do it again!"

"It's too late for that," Dee said. "You need to learn."

She started for the door. Just as she did, Caroline summoned some inner reserve of desperate strength, and lunged after her, reaching for her mother's arm. As her weight fell against the side rail, she heard the plastic and metal creak and groan, then snap. It fell away, broken, leaving Caroline momentarily suspended in the air between her mattress edge and the floor. She had a deranged thought—*I'm floating, I'm weightless*—then toppled to the ground, landing hard enough that she might have cracked her chin and knocked herself out had something not broken her fall.

Or rather, someone.

"Mama!" Caroline tried to push herself up but couldn't; that momentary strength had come and gone, leaving her as stranded as she had been that long-ago day at recess. She could feel Dee struggling beneath her, and pawed for the bed frame, knowing if she didn't move, Dee would smother beneath her weight. "Hang on, Mama," she pleaded. "I'm trying to move!"

But it was no use, nothing she could find to grab, nothing strong enough to help her gain leverage.

Toby's in the living room.

The thought filled her with horrified dismay. If she screamed, he'd come running, but then he'd see her. He'd find her lying on the ground, the back of her hospital-style gown wide open, no underpants beneath. Bare-assed, bare-legged, with her mother pinned beneath her — the boy she was in love with would see it all.

She began to cry again, then to scream, her voice hoarse and ragged. She didn't know his real name, but still she called for him. "Help us! Oh, God, please — hurry! *Help!*"

"Caroline…" Dee croaked.

"In here, please! Help us!"

"He…isn't there," Dee said. "He isn't there. He…never was…"

"What?" Caroline whispered, stunned. "What are you saying?"

Because as awful as it would have been had Toby been there, if he'd seen her, learned of her silly, childish infatuation, this was even worse.

Because it means we're all alone. No one is going to help.

The mattress whistled and whirred as the airflow shifted, and when it tipped in Caroline's direction, she saw the broken bed rail dangling down. It had dropped close enough so she could reach it if she tried; she could hook it with her hand and use it, if not to pull herself all the way off Dee, then enough to at least allow her mother to escape from beneath her.

"Mama!" She stretched out her hand, fingers splayed wide and desperate. "Mama, hang on! I...I think I can..."

Look at yourself.

All at once, she imagined Dee's voice, as clear and cold as if she'd spoken aloud.

He'll think you're disgusting, nothing more than a joke..

Caroline stared at the railing, tantalizingly within her reach. All she had to do was move just a little, no more than inches, and she could grab it. Still, she kept thinking of Dee's voice...

Look at yourself.

...of Dee buying her that chocolate cake after school, and all the times she'd shoveled spoonful after heaping spoonful of food onto her plate.

You have big bones. You need to eat this much. It's for your own good.

Why had Dee lied and said Toby had come over? That he was sitting in the very next room?

You know why, Caroline told herself. It was the same reason Dee would pinch her cheeks hard enough to leave a bruise, or why she'd never allowed Caroline to go outside and play with other children.

They'll laugh at you, just like the kids at school, remember?

Caroline let her hand fall to the floor, her mother's words resounding in her mind. Even though Dee had always tried to disguise the harsh things she'd say or do as endearments, there was no denying the bitter, awful truth: she was monstrous and cruel.

It's for your own good.

"Mama?"

She realized she could no longer feel Dee moving beneath her, however faint or feeble, and even though she strained to listen, Caroline couldn't hear her breathing.

"Mama? Oh...oh, God, Mama?"

Stretching her hand out again, gritting her teeth, sweat blooming across her brow with sudden, fervent determination, Caroline reached for the bed rail, seizing hold. As she clutched it, she prayed desperately for strength once more, pleading with the girl she wanted someday to be—who walked outside and rode her bike and had friends she could talk to, someone to love her—and with a ragged cry, she pulled herself sideways, falling away from Dee.

She could see her mother's face frozen in a dusky mask of tragedy, her features twisted and distorted. Her eyes remained open, glassy and bulging, her lips hanging ajar, a thin ribbon of drool trailing toward her chin.

"Oh, my God," Caroline gasped, clapping her hand over her mouth in horror. After a moment, she began to shudder as if with sobs, but when her hand fell away, only shrill peals of laughter escaped.

"Oh, my God," she cried, laughing until tears streamed down her cheeks and the bed adjusted again, the mattress shifting positions, pulling the railing from her grasp.

On her hands and knees, Caroline crawled toward the bedroom door. She couldn't remember the last time she'd seen more beyond that threshold than what the vantage from her bed allowed, but she meant to see it now, no matter how long it took to reach it.

Somewhere beyond that door, she'd find her mother's purse, and in it, Dee's phone; with it, she'd get help.

I'm going to get out of here, she thought, gritting her teeth, dragging herself forward. *Out of this room, this godforsaken house, and into the world.*

It was just like her mother had always said, perhaps the only truthful words Dee had ever uttered:

It's for my own good.

It Will Have Blood

"When was the last time this volcano erupted?" The woman's eyes cut nervously from me to the rocky slope in the distance, from which plumes of steam could be seen.

"I guess that depends on what you mean by eruption," I replied with a laugh that was meant to make her feel more at ease. Given the way her eyes widened, it had the opposite effect. "The last major eruption was back in 1924," I said, trying again. "Velada Island has only had intermittent smaller ones since then."

I could tell this didn't help either. The woman stepped back, rigid as a fencepost, clutching her gas mask in one hand, her husband's shirt sleeve in the other.

"It's alright, babe," he said with an apologetic smile and murmured thanks for me as I handed him a respirator. "Nothing to worry about."

She'd been one of the first of the tour group to complain once we'd hit the open water after leaving port, asking if we really needed to go so fast, because the speed and choppy seas were making people seasick. Not surprisingly, when I checked the roster on my clipboard, I saw her name was Karen.

"Velada's in a constant state of ventilation," Soto said as he hauled a plastic tote out of the Zodiac inflatable motorboat, dropping it onto the jetty. With the kind of wide, confident smile usually gifted only to movie stars and male models, he turned, pointing toward the crater. "See those steam clouds? They're releasing pressure from the magma chamber even as we speak. It's like loosening a relief valve on a pressure cooker. A little bit comes out over a long period of time and keeps the whole thing from blowing all at once."

It was hard not to be charmed by Soto when he was in full-on smarm mode like that, at least if you didn't know him—which I did. Karen didn't, however, so while I rolled my eyes behind the mirrored lenses of my sunglasses, the corners of her mouth fluttered up in a smile, her cheeks blooming with color.

"Oh," she said. "Oh, I see. That makes sense."

"Not only that, but you see that far ridge?" Now Soto stepped close enough to make her blush even more brightly as he pointed again. "The U.S. Geological Survey's got all kinds of cameras set up along there. They'd let us know if it wasn't safe."

There were cameras, yeah, and they might have been placed by the U.S. Geological Survey once upon a time, but as far as I knew, none of them worked and no one had used them in at least a decade.

"You're so full of shit," I told him as Karen and her husband followed the cragged length of the jetty to join the rest of our tour group.

He laughed. "You kiss your boyfriend with that mouth?"

"Why? You jealous?"

"Always," he said, dropping me a wink.

"Watch out for that guy," my preceptor had told me shortly after I'd been hired. "Alejandro Soto Morales. Goes by Soto. He's a real player, likes to sweettalk all the female guides, see how long it takes to fuck them."

Despite this warning, Soto had never once tried anything with me. I've never known whether to feel grateful or insulted.

The second Zodiac with passengers from the tour boat motored up to the jetty. We had fourteen visitors in all, divided into two groups: seven with me and Soto, the others with our coworkers, Ryan and Aubrey. While they disembarked onto the jetty, Soto carried our bins to the beach for safekeeping and I joined our group for last minute reminders and safety checks. I walked them through putting on the respirators and adjusting the masks to fit properly. Then Soto passed around yellow hard hats for everyone to wear, while I followed with a bowl of hard candies.

"Grab a few," I told everyone. "They're good to suck on as we go along. They help keep your mouth from getting too irritated by the fumes."

That aggravating worry flickered back into Karen's eyes. "Isn't that what the gas masks are for?"

"Yes, but you'll only need them closer to the crater," Soto explained. "On the way up, you might still notice the smell, feel a little dry mouth. Perfectly normal and harmless."

"Oh," she said, charmed yet again and taking several pieces. "Okay, then."

"Velada Island is the peak of an underwater volcano rising approximately three thousand, nine-hundred feet off the seafloor," I told the group as we followed a rugged path from the beach. "It's part of what's known as the Ring of Fire, a band of nearly one thousand volcanoes stretching all the way around the Pacific Ocean basin, and the only noncontiguous volcano of nearly thirty found in the state of California."

As I walked, I periodically glanced behind me to make sure everyone kept up and within earshot. Soto brought up the rear of the group, and I noticed a couple younger women had fallen back to walk closer to him. Although we recommend wearing comfortable clothes on the tour, they'd gone to the extreme with athletic leggings and matching tank tops, the kind that cling skin-tight and leave nothing to the imagination.

He's got to be loving this, I thought, rolling my eyes again behind my sunglasses as they paused now with Soto sandwiched between them. One held out her phone with one hand, flashing a peace sign with the other as she took a selfie. He had his arms around them and grinned, the proverbial tom cat with his hottie canaries.

Pathetic.

"Hey, Soto," I called, cock-blocking with a saccharine-sweet smile. "You with me?"

"Always."

"Good. How about you tell us about the sulfur features on Velada Island?"

"Of course," he said as he untangled himself from the women. "So, I'm sure everyone's had the chance by now to notice that rotten-egg smell in the air? I promise it's not just Kaila up there crop-dusting the rest of us with farts as she's leading the pack…"

Everyone laughed at this. I scratched the side of my nose with my middle finger, a gesture he didn't miss, judging by his grin.

"Sulfur gas is released when the magma beneath the volcano rises toward the surface and cools," he continued. "Every day, the crater releases hundreds, if not thousands of tons of sulfur gas. It's mixed with the steam…" He pointed ahead of us, the continuously billowing clouds. "…with the water in the crater lake you'll see in a few minutes, and it's leaching out of the ground under our feet. See the yellow crust everywhere? That's crystallized sulfur."

"In some places, those sulfur crystals build up the same way stalagmites do on the floors of cave systems," I added. "Over time, they grow tall, sometimes three feet or more."

I pointed out a cluster of these features as we rounded a slight bend. They were close enough to see but not touch, which was a good thing considering steam hissed and spat from ragged holes at the top of each pale protuberance. From another nearby vent, something else escaped: a viscous ooze that splattered to the ground, forming a wide, colorful pool of vermillion, orange, and yellow. The tourists oohed and aahed, coming to a collective stop and pulling out cell phones and cameras.

"It's so beautiful," I heard someone breathlessly exclaim.

"Like a painting," gasped another.

"It looks like blood," the woman, Karen, said. The strange comment caught me off guard, and I sputtered for a moment, trying to come up with a response.

"When it's molten, sulfur's red like that," Soto said. "As it cools, it lightens and eventually turns yellow. We'll pass several deposits like this as we go across the lahar."

"Lahar?" one of the tank-top twins repeated.

"That's what we're standing on." Soto tapped the toe of his hiking boot against the ground. "After the last big eruption in 1924, this entire side of the crater collapsed in a landslide. It got mixed in with water from the lake, plus all kinds of rocks and debris, and swept everything down to the sea. Over time, it hardened again, but left this incline along part of the island."

The trail grew steeper as we moved along, the heat that seeped up through the ground intensifying as we approached the peak. I found myself begrudgingly envious of the tank-top twins as I felt patches of sweat spreading between my shoulder blades and beneath my arms. Meanwhile, Soto continued talking to the group.

"…and on our way back down to the beach, we'll follow a trail on the other side of the crater. We'll pass by the ruins of the former Belknap Sulfur Mine, which was destroyed by the landslide in 1924. More than a dozen miners are presumed to have been killed. Their bodies were never found."

"Sulfur was mined from the surface of the crater," I added helpfully. "From deposits like the ones we saw earlier. Workers would go in by hand and chip off blocks of the sulfur crystals once they'd cooled. Between 1885 and 1900, more than five thousand tons were shipped to the mainland, where it was used in the production of sugar, gunpowder, matchsticks, and fertilizers."

I could have worn a blindfold and still known when we reached the top. Not only because we had everyone stop shortly before and put their respirators on, but because once we hit that crest and the breadth of the crater came fully into view — a sheer, straight plunge down to the steaming lake below — a reverent hush fell over them. It didn't last long, only a second or two, but those fleeting moments were my favorite parts of the job, the ones that brought me almost a giddy sort of glee, like I'd just shared a tremendous, wondrous secret that until that moment had been mine alone.

"Oh, my God," I heard someone say and then it was over, the silence broken, as one by one, they marveled.

"Don't get close to the edge," I called in reminder. "Remember, we can't stay long. The fumes are too strong here, even with the masks. We've got ten minutes, then…"

My voice faltered as I felt a sudden, curious tremor beneath my feet. I don't know if any of the tourists noticed it or not, but Soto must have, too, because he turned to me from the far side of the group, his expression quizzical.

"Wow," said a man, pointing at something beyond my shoulder. "Look at that."

As I turned, I heard more of the tourists murmur and gasp, their voices an excited chorus as a column of black smoke rose from the crater lake.

"How cool," one of the tank-top twosome said, turning around and raising her camera again to snap a selfie with it in the frame.

The ground beneath us shuddered again, and this time, everyone felt it. Even if they didn't, there was no missing the low grumble of grinding stone, or the way the base of the black smoke seemed to widen, spreading out like an enormous, dark bloom ready to unfurl.

I cut a glance at Soto again, saw the alarmed realization in his eyes, and knew we both understood what was about to happen.

"Run." I meant to shout in calm, confident imperative, to direct everyone toward the path again and from there to the beach, just like in our safety drills. Instead, my voice failed me, muffled by my respirator, and I reached up, pawing at it to try again.

"Run!" Soto beat me to it, jerking his own mask down. "Everybody, head to the beach. Now — right now, run!"

Confused and frightened, people started to move like a bewildered flock of chickens, without any clear purpose or direction. They stumbled about, turning this way and that, and it wasn't until another shockwave rolled underfoot, the strongest yet, that everyone seemed galvanized into action.

"*Run!*" I screamed. "It's an eruption! Go, go, go!"

At that word — *eruption* — people finally got it. Shrieking now, they began to flee, stumbling over the loose rocks and gravel on the ground, slipping and falling, then staggering upright once more. As we raced from the crater, I felt Soto grab my hand, and we ran together, the tourists scattered ahead of us, throwing panic-stricken looks back over their shoulders. Whatever they saw there, whatever made their eyes widen even more in abject terror, I didn't dare turn around to see.

Everything around us suddenly grew dim, as if twilight had started to settle eight hours early. I knew it wasn't that, though, but rather, the pyroclastic cloud — whatever enormous, hellish swell of black smoke and ash that had burst free from the mountain's belly — was now swallowing the sun and sky. Any second now, it would swallow us, too, I realized in horror. Expanding not just upwards but out, it would catch up to us at any moment, engulf us.

I thought of my mom, because that's what you do when you're about to die, right? I thought about Mom and how when I'd last talked to her, she'd fretted for at least the millionth time about my job.

"I just don't think it's safe," she'd said. "I mean, on clear days, I'm told you can see smoke from that thing all the way at San Pedro."

"It's not smoke, Mom. It's steam," I'd told her, going on to offer her the same placating bullshit Soto had offered poor, nervous Karen earlier. Not because I meant to lie, not on purpose or anything, but because I hadn't wanted her to worry. I'd thought there was nothing to worry about.

The looming shadow grew darker, and I could hear it now over the rumbling as the earth shook: the roar of the approaching cloud. A hard rain began to fall, chunks of rock and pumice plummeting from the sky, some of it still burning, smashing against the ground all around us. I tripped, then fell. Soto skittered to a stop, then rushed back, dragging me to my feet. We ran again, but the air lay choked with dust and smoke. We'd lost sight of the tour group, not to mention the trail, and I had no idea where we were going or how much time we had left. Surely, it was only seconds —

I felt the ground beneath my feet suddenly give way, like a layer of thin ice over a winter pond yielding. Instead of icy water beneath, I felt only open air, and I had less than a second to yelp Soto's name before we both fell, plunging into a chasm that had opened in the earth. I never thought I'd be thankful for the ugly fucking hard hat we had to wear, but as I ricocheted off first one cragged surface, then another, I was grateful as hell, because without it, I'm sure my skull would have been pulverized.

I slammed belly-first against the ground and heard a heavy thud as Soto hit somewhere close by. Then, whatever sunlight may have been seeping down through the hole above us was abruptly gone, snuffed entirely as the pyroclastic cloud roared overhead. We were plunged into sudden, absolute, impenetrable darkness, and all I was aware of was a sound like a freight train barreling past, and the terrifying, seemingly endless shaking of the earth.

I clamped my eyes shut and curled my body into a ball, waiting for whatever searing wind that might make it down that narrow shaft to find us, roast us alive, but it never came. Only darkness and that terrible bellow that seemed like it would never end.

And then it did.

Everything fell silent, a quiet so profound and oppressive, you could feel it inside your head the way pressure built up as you sank in the deep end of a swimming pool. Darkness remained, but no longer complete; pale, fluttering hints of glow trickled down from the hole above us, sunlight winking in and out of view through the smoke.

Every bruise, scrape, and laceration I'd sustained in the fall began coming to life, blooming painfully into my awareness. I peeled my eyelids open, squinting against the sting of ash and fumes, watching an eerie cascade of tiny flower petals fluttering down through the hole.

No, I thought dimly because that wasn't right, couldn't possibly be. There were no plants on Velada Island, no life of any sort.

Ash, I thought. The last of whatever the volcano had vomited into the sky, pale and delicate particles that danced and whirled as they floated down.

I heard Soto groan and sat up slowly. Within the waxing, waning measure of sunlight, I saw him lying on the ground less than five feet away. He'd landed on his back and remained like that, arched slightly because of the backpack pinned beneath him.

Moving slowly, grimacing as I did, I unslung my own backpack, then fumbled with the zippers, my hands shaking and unsteady. I pawed around inside until I found my flashlight and turned it on, its wide, bright beam, dispelling some of the darkness.

"Soto?" I also pulled out my first aid kit from the pack and crawled toward him. "Soto? Can you hear me? Wake up."

His eyelids fluttered, and he blinked up at me, dazed.

"H-hey." Reaching beneath my chin, I unbuckled the straps of my hard hat and pulled it off so he could see my face better. "It's me, Kaila."

He nodded, his eyes drooping closed again, and I felt a surge of alarm. "Hey," I said, shaking him by the shoulders. "You with me, Soto?"

Another sleepy nod. "Always."

I removed his hard hat, then helped him sit up. To my dismay, I saw a large bloodstain on the back of his T-shirt, and the ground where he'd been lying was soaked.

"Soto...!" I gasped as he fell against me.

"'s alright," he mumbled into the front of my T-shirt. "I'm...okay..."

I pulled off his backpack and laid him down again, rolling him onto his side. When I pulled back the bloody hem of his shirt, I sucked in a sharp breath to see a deep, ragged gash torn from just below his shoulder to the crest of his hip.

"I'm okay," he said again, and when he tried to move, blood swelled up and out of that gruesome, meaty cleft.

"No, you're not, you dumbass." I pushed him down again. "Be still."

I dug through the first-aid kit but the best I could find were a couple of large combine pads and a roll of gauze. Holding the pads in place, I pressed down as hard as I could manage, trying to slow his blood loss. Next, I reached around him in an awkward embrace, wrapping the gauze around his torso to bind the wound.

He shook slightly and made a soft sound at this. It took me a second to realize he was laughing.

"What the hell's so funny?" I demanded. "You're hurt, stupid. I'm trying to help you."

"I know. It's just…I've always pictured this the other way around: me…all up on you…from behind…"

I blinked in surprise. "You…you…" I sputtered, then slapped his arm. "You asshole."

He laughed again, even though it obviously hurt. "I'm sorry."

"I mean, seriously? You pick *now* to try and hit on me?"

"Might not…get another chance…"

I paused, my arms still around him, the gravity of his words sinking in. "Don't talk like that," I whispered. "It's going to be alright."

Once his dressings were in place, I laid him back, using his pack as a makeshift pillow. "Where are we?" he asked, craning his head to look around.

"I think it's an empty sulfur vent," I said. "We must've fallen through an old chimney when the ground caved in."

I hobbled to my feet, shining the light in front of me, surprised and unnerved by just how far it traveled before reaching the far side of the chamber. The wall glittered as the beam swept across it, sulfur crystals coating it like thick frost.

"It's big," I said, panning the light around. "Really big. This must've been a huge sulfur pool at some point. I wonder what—"

Just then, my light swept past the unmistakable shapes of a human ribcage and skull and startled, I let out a shriek.

"What is it?" Soto said. "What's wrong?"

"Bones," I said, letting the flashlight crawl now across not just one skeleton sprawled at the base of the far wall, but several. One…two…three…I tried to keep track as the light went past, and with each one I counted, my confusion and fear mounted. "There are skeletons down here. Six of them."

"Let me see," he said, struggling to sit up.

"Lie down," I said and when he started to argue, I snapped, "You want to start bleeding again? You know there's at least three hours before anyone from the mainland can get here to help. You'll be dead way before then if you don't lie still."

It sounded harsh, and I felt bad, but it remained the truth, and it worked. Realizing I was right, or at least giving in, Soto sagged back against his makeshift pallet.

Turning my attention back to the skeletons, I approached cautiously. "Who were they, do you think?"

"Maybe the miners? The ones from a hundred years ago. No one ever found their bodies."

It made sense. If some had fallen through the same sort of cave-in we had, and the mudslide following the eruption had buried the opening, they would have been trapped down here, buried for God only knew how long until they starved to death or died of thirst.

Or ran out of air, I thought with a shudder.

Whoever they were, the remains had been down there a long time. That much became obvious the closer I approached, because like the walls, the skeletons had been covered in a fine layer of sulfur crystals, a sparkling yellow crust that now cemented them to the ground. As I panned my light around cautiously, looking for any others, I noticed something else along the far wall. With a curious frown, I limped in that direction.

"It shouldn't take hours for help to reach us," I heard Soto say. "There's a Naval base on San Nicolas Island. That's only fifteen miles or so south of here…a half-hour, tops by boat. They'll have seen the smoke from the eruption. They'll send help."

"You're so full of shit," I told him. "The only thing the Navy does on San Nicolas is weapons testing. The whole island's unoccupied."

Soto would know this, of course. I realized he'd said it for my benefit, just like he'd told the tourist Karen about the cameras on the crater ridge, even though they no longer worked. Because he hadn't wanted me to worry.

"But help's still coming, either way," I said, raising my light as I turned to face him. "We're going to—"

Get out of this, okay? was what I meant to say, but my voice cut short as the ground beneath us gave another of those low, terrible rumbles.

I felt sudden panic, wondering if the mountain wasn't finished with us yet, if now it meant to erupt again or, worse, send another landslide careening down to bury us here, just as it had the miners.

"Kaila...?" Soto's voice sounded raspy, like he gasped for breath, and I realized he'd pulled his respirator away so he could raise his head, look for me.

"I'm okay," I said. "Put your mask back on."

"What are you doing?"

"There's something here, a hole in the wall," I said, taking a closer look at what had distracted me just before the tremor. "I think it must be part of the old vent shaft system."

It was wide enough so that I could've crawled through it and investigated if I wanted. I couldn't tell how deep it went, but the downward grade of the shaft was obvious.

"Is it a way out, do you think?" He sounded weaker now, and his breathing had taken on a ragged, hitching quality I didn't like. I'd slowed his bleeding down, at least temporarily, but he was still in bad shape. I didn't have time for distractions.

"No, it goes down, probably deeper into the mountain." When I returned to him, I could see blood seeping through the thick pads and gauze covering his wounds. "I'm going to try and climb out of here."

"I...I can help..." he began, but when he tried to move, I placed my palm against his shoulder.

"I've got this, alright? You just lie here and rest. I'll have you out in no time."

He managed a feeble laugh. "And you always say *I'm* full of shit."

I left the light with him and approached the shaft, looking at the patch of sky overhead. I stretched up my hands, feeling along the rough surface of the walls, searching for divots. Slowly, painfully, I began to climb, inching my way toward the top. I nearly made it, no more than a foot or two from the surface, when from beneath me, I heard it again, that ominous groan from deep inside the volcano, and felt the first thready shivers of another quake through my fingertips.

Shit!

Just as I splayed my hands and feet wide, digging in to brace myself, the tremors hit again. As miniature avalanches of ash, pumice, and gravel rained down at me, my hands lost purchase first, then my boot soles. I uttered a frightened cry as I crashed back down toward the chamber floor, my voice snapping short as an outcropping of rock slammed into my side, sending enough pain searing through me to knock me nearly out cold.

I only dimly remember landing, my consciousness ebbing and flowing like the tide. I could hear Soto's frightened voice, calling my name, then found myself blinking up at him, bleary-eyed.

"Kaila," he exclaimed. "Don't move. Are you hurt?"

"I…I'm fine."

The ground had stopped shaking, but even so, we could still hear that low, visceral grumbling, like distant thunder from an approaching stormfront.

"Help me…sit up," I said, and when he did, I bit back a cry as best I could. I know he heard me nonetheless, and when he held me in his arms, as if trying to clumsily comfort me, I could see his dressings had soaked through with blood.

"I...I need to try again," I said, and he shook his head.

"No. You're hurt—"

"I *have* to!" I cried, because I was watching him bleed to death before my eyes, goddamn it. How could I stop? How could I not try again? I pushed him away, then staggered to my feet. "I can make it, Soto. I can make it to the top, and I...I'll get help...I..."

Just as my voice broke, I heard a sound from behind us, coming from the strange hole in the wall. As I turned to look, Soto picked up the flashlight and directed its beam toward the far corner of the chamber.

"What the fuck...?" he whispered, which meant he could see it, too, and it wasn't my imagination, the stream of what appeared to be blood suddenly flowing out of the shaft's opening. Dark and glistening, you could only tell it was red when the light met it directly, but there was no mistaking that it was somehow defying gravity and *flowing uphill*, burbling out of the hole, spreading in a widening pool across the chamber floor.

Is that...sulfur?

We both recoiled, because of course, it was sulfur—there wasn't anything else it could be—and it was flowing red in a liquid state, meaning it was molten, as hot as lava.

"Shit! The quakes must've reopened the shaft somehow." Looking up, I surveyed the rock walls again, already eying the handholds and notches I'd used before.

"I'll go back to the beach. There were ropes in one of the totes we took off the Zodiac."

"Kaila," Soto said.

"It won't take long," I promised without looking back, already reaching up and digging my fingertips in, readying to pull myself up. "I can make it this time. And I'm a fast runner. I was on the track team in high school. Did I ever tell you that?"

"Kaila…"

"The two-hundred meter dash, that's what I ran. I even—"

"*Kaila.*"

The sharpness in his voice, the urgency, stopped me cold and I turned to him in a slow, stumbling circle.

And saw it.

Emerging from the mouth of the sulfur shaft, the hot, crimson liquid rolling off like water from a goose's back, was something I'd never seen before, whether inside my worst nightmares or in the real world, where such things weren't supposed to exist. Its shape was vaguely human, its misshapen head too large to balance against the elongated stalk of its neck. It was transparent—not translucent like the frosted glass of a shower door, but rather completely see-through like a windowpane, its outline and contours only discernable by the wink of reflected light off its surface. Beneath this clear, outer sheath, I could see organs floating, not the systematic arrangements found in human anatomy illustrations, but something chaotic and random, as if thrown together by a madman: a pulsating mass of pinkish flesh here, a misshapen twist of greyish tissue there. I saw no nervous system, blood vessels, or bones, only this haphazard collection of pieces and parts, miscellaneous meat suspended in gelatinous ooze.

As it slogged through the broadening pool of steaming, melted sulfur, it extended a pair of what looked like human arms, only impossibly, monstrously long. Behind these, more appendages twitched and writhed, some human in appearance, others pliable like tentacles, others still that were more segmented and insectile.

Eyeballs floated inside the vitreous humor of its head, at least a dozen of them, human eyes with flimsy scraps of muscle still attached, all turning and pivoting without anchors or sockets, the frayed filaments of severed optic nerves trailing behind. Beneath these, like some sort of jellyfish bobbing up and down, I saw at least three complete human brains, with remnants of spinal cords dangling impotently beneath.

"Wh-what is that?" Soto whispered.

"I don't know," I whispered back.

"But...you see it, right?" He looked over his shoulder at me. "What in Christ's name...in the actual fuck...*is it?*"

"I don't know," I said again, but there were two things I *did* know with sudden, terrifying certainty: first, whatever it was, it was crawling *straight for us,* and second, I did *not* want to find out what would happen if it reached us. "You have to get up. We're getting out of here."

He didn't argue with me, clearly having no desire to find out more about the fucking thing, either. I heard him choke back a cry as I helped to his feet, then the two of us leaned together.

"You're going to have to climb," I told him grimly, and he nodded. "You go first, okay? I'll tell you where to grab hold."

He shook his head. "I'll only slow us down. And if I fall…"

We both cut anxious glances behind us. By now the thing from the sulfur shaft had made it halfway across the chamber. It seemed to either be exercising caution or curiosity in our regard, in no particular hurry either way. Maybe it had been hibernating, I thought, and we'd roused it somehow; maybe it was slow because it was still drowsy, then, and we might have a chance to escape.

It kept its many eyes riveted on us. A strange, high-pitched sound like a chorus of cicadas or frogs seemed to emanate from it, but I couldn't discern any distinguishable lips or mouth.

"You go first," Soto told me, and even though I knew he was right, I hated myself for admitting it.

"Okay," I whispered. Then, narrowing my brows, I added, "Watch where I put my hands and feet, then you do the same. When I get to the top, I'll help pull you all the way up."

He nodded, then we were off. If I'd thought it hurt before trying to scale that chimney after having previously tumbled down it, the second time around was even worse. I couldn't go very fast, but Soto could barely keep up at all and I kept looking back to make sure he hadn't fallen too far behind.

"I'm fine," he rasped, his shoulders trembling from exertion. "Keep...going."

Below him, I saw movement, then that shrill buzzing grew louder as the creature thrust its head into view.

"Soto—!" I cried, as its tangle of arms and arachnoid legs suddenly pushed up and around its head, pawing and scrabbling along the sides of the shaft. Whatever fatigue I'd either sensed or imagined in it earlier was gone; it moved with terrifying speed and purpose now, wriggling back and forth, trying to squeeze itself into the narrow confines and climb after us.

"Go!" Soto yelled, and I could hear the terror in his voice, see it in his eyes. I forced myself to move, to reach for the next indentation in the stone, then the next one, and the next, pulling my feet up beneath me as I went, kicking my toes into these same shallow places to bear my weight. All at once, I felt reverberations in the shaft walls again, like the resonant thrumming of a guitar string that's been plucked.

Oh, God, I thought, because I knew it meant another aftershock, one that could potentially entomb us here together: me, Soto, and that godforsaken thing.

"Soto—" I began, looking back to warn him. A clear, gelatinous filament had risen toward his leg, curling loosely around his boot. He hadn't noticed it yet, but did now as I screamed, my terror of the creature eclipsing even that of the volcano.

Before he could react, the slender proboscis drew taut, latching onto him. He started to fall, then thrust his hands out to stop, kicking his free foot out and planting it against the wall. The creature below pulled with unimaginable force, crushing his boot like it was made of tissue paper. I heard the sickening, wet crunch as his ankle splintered and Soto bit back a scream, the tendons standing out taut and strained in his arms and neck.

"Go, Kaila," he cried, just as more of those thread-like appendages encircled his legs and waist, yanking him down.

"*Soto!*" I shrieked as he fell.

We'd abandoned the flashlight when we'd started to climb, and by its fading glow as dirt and rocks rained down on it, I saw Soto and the creature crash to the ground together, Soto on his back, sprawled on top of it. He uttered a cry, and as he tried to sit up, I could see it burning him somehow, its deceptively benign flesh blistering his like acid. He began sinking into its soft, viscous form, not as much being enveloped by its body as absorbed.

"No," he cried, clawing desperately at the open air, struggling to escape. "No, no, get it off me, goddamn it, *get it —* "

His voice cut short as, with a thick, moist squelch, the creature swallowed him whole. I could see him floating inside of it; he jerked several times, shuddered, then fell still as if paralyzed. His eyes rolled frantically, the only parts he could still control or move, and blood bloomed around him in a murky cloud. Before it obscured his face from view, I watched his skin pull loose from the underlying meat and muscle of his cheek and jaw, dangling like Spanish moss, melting away — *dissolving.*

"Soto...!" I wailed, feeling bile rise in my throat. "Oh...oh, God..."

My feet started sliding as the quaking increased, and I felt a wild moment of bright, primal alarm as I scrambled to stop myself from falling. Below, I saw that fucking thing's hideous head fill the base of the shaft again, all of its horrible eyes focused on me. The drone of cicadas suddenly became a deafening screech, and again, it lunged upward, cramming itself into the shaft.

I screamed, then started to climb, clawing at the rock walls until my nails ripped off and my fingertips bled. Larger sections of stone began falling now as the sides began to crumble—and worse, the hole above me started to cave in.

"No!" I raced for it, watching in dismay as the circle of sunshine and blue sky above me began shrinking in circumference, the shaft collapsing. I felt something graze my foot from below, and with a shriek, I kicked and kicked until it fell away.

"No," I sobbed. "No, God, no, *please!*"

My fingers scrabbled out of the top of the hole, then I scrambled up, my body seized with adrenaline, desperation, and despair. I managed to haul myself to the surface split seconds before the shaft completely collapsed with a thunderous roar, rocks and debris falling to fill the empty space I'd only just barely escaped. I lay in the dirt, gasping for breath, the last of the tremors fading to stillness beneath me.

Soto...

It had been eating him. Worse than watching him bleed to death in front of me, I'd watched him being digested—*dissolved*—and this realization was too much, too horrible for me to bear. I managed to push myself up before vomiting into the dust and ash, the wrenching of my gut nothing next to that of my heart.

After that, there was nothing more I could do besides wait. I didn't have the strength to try and make it to the beach. Instead, I crawled until I reached the shelter of a nearby rocky outcropping, then hid beneath it in the shade. I tasted blood in my mouth, the sour tang of spent bile, and the bitter saltiness of my tears.

Help is coming, I told myself as I closed my eyes. I imagined Soto's voice, his words, his face, his smile.

There's the Naval base on San Nicolas Island. That's only fifteen miles or so...half-hour, tops by boat. They'll have seen the smoke from the eruption. They'll send help.

I tried to pretend the faint sound I heard even now through the ground—like a nest of cicadas buried deep and shrieking—was all in my mind, that this was somehow nothing more than a nightmare, the worst sort from which I'd wake up and be free from at any moment.

Don't worry, I imagined Soto saying, whispering to me in promise. *Help will be here soon.*

You've Been Saved

"Remember the time Mikey busted us into his uncle's house to get that fifth of Jack Daniels he swore was hidden underneath the kitchen sink?"

Using nothing but his driver's permit, Chris Flynn thought as his friend, Ethan Brooks said this aloud.

"Using nothing but his goddamn driver's permit, you remember that? He jimmies it between the door and the jamb..."

Gives it a wiggle or two to wedge it underneath the bolt... Chris thought.

"...then he gives it a shake," Ethan said. "Once, twice..."

...three time's the charm, because...

"...the next thing I hear is that bolt going *POP* as the lock comes undone, and he's opening the door with this big, shit-eating grin on his face."

All of that, and there's not a goddamn thing under that sink. Do you...

"...remember that, Chris? Nothing but a bunch of old, dried-up mouse shit!" Ethan slapped his hand against the table and laughed loudly enough to draw glances from people at neighboring seats in the roadside diner. "Goddamn, those were good times."

One hour into their cross-country trek to Los Angeles spent recounting "good times" had been fun for Chris. Two hours listening to Ethan's stories had been mostly enjoyable, and three hours of it, moderately so. After five hours, however, Chris's patience had worn thin. By now, ten hours deep, and another nineteen yet to go—not including the overnight detour they'd planned in Las Vegas—and he found himself ready to impale himself on his fork.

"You boys need anything else?" Short and stout, their waitress wore her cinnamon-colored hair teased high and a shade too bright to be natural. Her nametag read *Lois*.

"Just the check, please," Chris said.

Lois pulled out her ticket pad. "Everything taste okay?"

Ethan smiled at her disarmingly. "Just like Mom used to make."

"You poor thing." She ripped off the bill, plopped it down on the table, then walked away.

While Ethan took care of the tab, Chris headed for the men's room. As he reached for the door, the adjacent one to the ladies' room swung open unexpectedly. Startled, he danced backwards as a young woman plowed nearly headlong into him.

"I'm sorry...!" she exclaimed in a startled, breathless rush, just as an older woman walked out behind her.

"Oh, my goodness, Jessie," she scolded. "Watch where you're going! You nearly knocked him over." With an apologetic smile, she added to Chris, "I'm so sorry. Are you alright?"

"I...I'm fine, ma'am," he replied, looking at the girl, Jessie, as he spoke. She was pretty enough to warrant more than a passing glance, with long, dark hair drooping in lank waves to her shoulders. The spaghetti straps of her white tank top were loose enough to promise no bra beneath, and a pair of low-slung blue jeans hugged the shapely curves of her hips.

"Come along now." The older woman caught Jessie by the crook of her elbow like she might have a naughty kid. "Let the young man by."

"It's alright…" Chris began, but his voice faltered as Jessie brushed past him, catching him by the hand. It was only for a second, but that was all she needed to press something into his palm, a wadded napkin she'd been carrying.

"Hey, man," Ethan called from the direction of the cash register. "You got fifteen cents?"

Chris looked down at the napkin, puzzled, then watched the older woman lead Jessie out of the diner. She glanced back at Chris, her dark eyes round and nearly pleading.

"Hey," Ethan said again, and this time, he reached over and punched Chris in the shoulder to get his attention. "Ground control to Major Tom. I asked if you've got fifteen cents. I don't want to bust a dollar."

"Uh, yeah. Sure." Reaching into the front pocket of his jeans, Chris pulled out some loose change. "Here."

Through one of the nearby windows, he could see Jessie and the woman crossing the parking lot together for an older model Winnebago. He and Ethan had both noticed it upon their arrival at the diner, if not because it was something straight out of a 1980s time capsule, perfectly, hideously preserved, then because of a bumper sticker on the vehicle's tail end: *HONK if you've been SAVED!*

Ethan had found this hilarious. "We should get one of those, a button or something you could wear at the hospital," he'd said, then busted out laughing. "Every time one of your patients rolls out of surgery, you could pinch them in the nose. You know…" And he'd demonstrated this on Chris. "Honk! You've been saved!"

While Ethan finished paying the bill, Chris looked down at the napkin Jessie had handed to him. It had been folded neatly and deliberately, the way notes were in grade school when students tried to surreptitiously pass them during class. Curious, he worked the edges loose and opened it.

HELP

The word, all caps and clumsy block letters, looked like it had been scrawled in blood. He cut his gaze again toward the diner window and watched the RV pull away, heading back for the interstate.

"What's that?" Ethan asked, pushing his wallet back into his pocket.

"I don't know," Chris replied, showing it to him.

"Where'd you get it?"

"That girl gave it to me a second ago."

Ethan frowned. "What girl?"

"The one in the tank top." With a pointed glance, Chris added, "No bra."

"Oh, yeah." Ethan handed the note back. "Well, that's weird."

"Yeah." Chris frowned as the Winnebago drove off. "You think she's in trouble?"

"Could be." Ethan blew a sour belch against the side of his fist and grimaced. "Especially if she had the lunch special, too."

***

"Maybe we should call the police," Chris said a half an hour later, when they were back on the road. He'd brought the note with him from the diner, and time and again, found himself glancing down at it, drawn to the grim plea, those stark, crooked letters.

HELP

"What the hell for?" Ethan asked.

"What if she's been kidnapped?" Chris asked, and when Ethan rolled his eyes, he frowned. "What? You hear about human trafficking all the time on the news."

"Yeah? You hear about people getting punked, too." Ethan grabbed the note and crumpled it up. When he opened the window, moving to toss it out, Chris grabbed his arm.

"Hey, don't."

But Ethan opened his hand anyway. The wind, whipping past the side of the car at more than seventy miles-an-hour, snatched the note and whipped it away.

"What the hell, man?" Chris exclaimed. "Why'd you do that?"

"Because it's bullshit, Chris," Ethan replied, rolling his window back up. "That girl was just messing around. Would you forget about it already?"

But that was easier said than done, at least for Chris. As the day wore on, he tried to feign the appropriate interest as Ethan talked about their Vegas side-trip, but still couldn't quite shake his nagging, lingering unease.

"...so, I'm thinking we should go to the Sahara first," Ethan said. "Hit the craps tables, you know, maybe play a little blackjack, then check out the nudie bars. I've heard there's a bunch of them all lined up in a row. Trust me, man. A nice pair of double-D's waving in your face is exactly what the doctor..." His voice faded and he frowned, leaning forward to look out the windshield. "Isn't that the same RV we saw back at the diner?"

"Where?"

"Right there." Ethan pointed ahead of them, toward the unmistakable brown-and-white Winnebago. "That is the same one. *HONK if you've been SAVED!*" His frown deepened. "Are you following them?"

"What? Don't be a dumbass." Chris feigned obliviousness. After all, the RV had held a good fifteen, if not twenty minute lead ahead of them on the highway. But head start or not, it had apparently hit a cruising speed of less than the posted limit, so he figured it wasn't completely his fault they'd caught up to it.

"A dumbass, huh?" Ethan said as the Winnebago's right turn signal came on when it neared an exit and Chris did the same.

"What? We need to fill up."

At the gas station, the RV pulled around the far side of the building toward bays designed for tractor trailers and other large vehicles. Chris rolled to a stop next to the regular pumps.

"Have you been following them this whole time?" Ethan demanded, annoyed now, folding his arms across his chest.

"Of course not."

"Good. Because I told you, that girl was just fucking with you." Ethan unfastened his seatbelt and reached for the car door. "I'm going to go take a piss. You want anything? A Coke? Some Cheeto's to go with your paranoia?"

"Yeah," Chris replied, flipping him the bird. "Ha, ha."

The afternoon sun was bright, the air dry and warm. He stood in the shade beneath the fueling island's overhang, trying to keep an eye on the Winnebago while letting the pump in his hand run. He watched as an older man got out on the driver's side to refill the camper while the woman crossed the parking lot for the convenience store. There was no sign of Jessie.

Out of the corner of his eye, he saw Ethan leave the store. To his bewildered surprise, rather than head back for their rental car, instead he strode boldly toward the Winnebago.

What is he doing?

The older man had been walking back to the driver's side door, but paused, turning when Ethan called out to him.

Shit, Chris thought, an inward groan. *Ethan, what the fuck are you doing?*

While he watched, Ethan chatted with the man, smiling broadly and offering sweeping gestures with his hands now and again to indicate the camper. When the woman emerged from the store, she, too, apparently exchanged introductions with Ethan. Then, with a flip of his hand in an affable wave, he strolled languidly back across the parking lot.

"Honk," he told Chris as he approached. "You've been saved, man."

"What the hell?" Chris exclaimed. "What were you doing?"

"I told you. Saving your ass," Ethan replied, opening a bottle of iced tea he'd bought and taking a long swig. "I wanted to prove to you that note was bullshit, so I went and talked to those folks. Their names are Bill and Libby Warner. Turns out, they're on the way back from a Bible convention in Utah. I told them my dad used to have an RV, and we'd travel all over the country every summer when I was a kid. Great Lakes, the Grand Canyon, Yellowstone, Disneyland — you name it."

Chris frowned. "Your dad didn't have an RV. He drove that piece of shit Buick."

"I know that," Ethan replied. "But *they* didn't. Anyway, they told me they like to travel around, too. Only they didn't have any kids to go with them. They never had any, you see." He took another swig of tea and glanced pointedly at Chris. "No kids," he said again.

"What about Jessie?"

Ethan shook his head. "I don't know. But the way they were talking, there's nobody else but the two of them."

They sat in the car for a long, quiet moment, with Chris relaxing, then tightening his grasp repeatedly on the steering wheel. Finally, with an aggravated sigh, he reached for the ignition. Ethan caught him by the wrist.

"This isn't about your dad, Chris," he said quietly.

Chris tried to laugh. "What? Where the hell did that come from? This doesn't have anything to do with my father."

"I know. I just said that."

"Then we're in agreement," Chris said, jerking his hand free so he could start the car. "So shut the fuck up, alright?"

He tried to maintain a careful distance between the car and the camper once they were underway again, if only to keep from rousing Ethan's suspicions once more. When the RV next turned off the highway, it was nearly dusk, and Chris again followed. The Winnebago stopped at a campground, while he pulled into the parking lot of a motel across the street.

"What's up? I thought you wanted to drive straight through." Ethan had been catnapping in the passenger seat and winced as he sat up, blinking dazedly at the buzzing neon *VACANCY* sign flashing overhead.

"I changed my mind." Chris killed the engine and unbuckled his seatbelt. "I'm beat."

"Oh." Ethan shrugged once, then dubiously surveyed the front of the motel. "You couldn't find a Holiday Inn or something? This place looks like a shit hole."

Chris laughed. "No, it doesn't."

"Come on, man. Seriously? I can practically feel the bedbugs from here."

"Would you stop? My back's killing me. I need to get out of this car. Besides, we've got beer that's been in the cooler all day, remember?" Chris leaned over and pinched Ethan's nose. "Honk, man. We've been saved."

Ethan laughed, slapping his hand away. "Right on."

◆

Once they'd checked in, Ethan stretched out on the bed, an opened beer bottle in hand and pay-per-view porno muted on the television while he called the latest in his endless string of girlfriends-de-jour.

"Is that the one from Christmas?" Chris asked when he'd hung up. "What was her name? Ellen?"

"You mean Erin? God, no. She didn't make it past Easter. This one's Melissa."

Polishing off a beer of his own, Chris tossed the bottle into the waste can, then rooted through the mostly melted ice chips to fish out another one.

"If you came around more often, you might know these things," Ethan remarked as Chris handed him a dripping bottle.

"I've been kind of busy."

"Yeah, I've noticed," Ethan said, twisting the cap off his beer. With a smile, he leaned forward, tapping his bottle neck into Chris's. "So how about you? Still seeing that one girl, the redhead?"

"Meredith? No." Tipping his head back, Chris took a swallow of beer. "She didn't last past Easter, either."

"What happened?"

Chris shrugged. "I've been kind of busy," he said again.

"Too busy for your friends," Ethan mused. "Too busy to keep a girl. Man, don't you ever get lonely?"

"I'm too busy." With a laugh, Chris took another long drink of beer. Because Ethan didn't laugh along with him, studying him instead as if he had those X-ray-vision sunglasses advertised in the back of old Spider-Man comics, he sighed. "Okay, fine. Yeah. Sometimes. Maybe. I don't know. Seriously, man. I don't have time to notice anymore."

"You think when you move out to California, you might find some?" Ethan asked. "Time, I mean."

"Not likely." Chris chuckled as he reclined against the headboard, his legs stretched out. "But I haven't got the cardiology fellowship yet. My interview's on Friday at UCLA."

"You'll get it, man. They'd be fucking nuts not to give it to you."

Chris glanced at him, oddly touched. "Thanks."

"Hey." Ethan shrugged, taking a swig of beer. "I know you've been busting your ass these past few years with medical school and everything. You're really doing alright. I always knew you would." Balancing the cap from his bottle against the pad of his thumb and using his index finger, he flicked it away, sending it flying toward the far corner of the room. "Just like I always knew I wouldn't."

"Bullshit," Chris said, but Ethan only shrugged again. "You're doing just fine."

Ethan mimed jerking himself off. "I'm the manager of a goddamn appliance store."

"Hey, I couldn't sell that shit."

"Yeah, because you're busy doing what, brain surgery?"

"Hearts," Chris corrected.

"Whatever. At least it matters. You don't show up for work, and someone could drop dead. *HONK, you've been SAVED,* remember? Me, I skip out, and some Susie Dipshit Homemaker's gotta ask another clerk to help her pick out a goddamn matching washer-dryer set."

"Ethan…" Chris said, reaching out, touching his shoulder gently.

"What you do makes a difference." Ethan shrugged him away, his expression growing somewhat sorrowful as he polished off his beer. "*You* make a difference." With a glance, he added, "I'm proud of you, man."

Chris smiled. "Thanks."

Ethan cut him a glance. "And I've missed you, goddamn it."

Chris clapped him on the shoulder again, fondly. "Yeah, man. Me, too."

◆

He dreamed that he was home again. Not the sparsely furnished apartment he seldom used for more than showering or changing his clothes, but the house he'd grown up in, his childhood home in the Bridgeport district of Chicago.

He heard a loud, sudden THUMP, something heavy hitting the floor. "Dad?" he called, because his mother had already left for work. He was twelve years old, an eighth grader at Saint Mary of the Angels, and it was his father's job to drive him to school every morning.

"Dad?"

He should have known, should have realized, should have *remembered*, but in the surreal world of the dream, he didn't. Instead, he went downstairs, curious but not necessarily alarmed. That is, until he saw his father lying face-down in the foyer.

"Dad!" Chris rushed down the stairs, taking them two and three at a time. It still hadn't occurred to him that he was a grown man now, not an adolescent boy. He didn't think about that, didn't think about anything, and instead, simply acted.

"Dad!" Grasping him by the shoulders, Chris turned him onto his back, then slid his fingertips beneath the fleshy shelf of his chin, searching for a pulse.

"Dad, hold on." Ripping open the front of his father's shirt, he exposed the white, soft bulge of his belly. Lacing his fingers together, he pushed the heel of one hand atop the graying strands of wiry hair nestled over his dad's sternum. "Hold on," he said again, straightening his arms, leaning forward to begin chest compressions. "I can fix this, Dad. I can fix it, just hold on."

◆

He woke with a start and a throbbing headache. The digital bedside clock read 5:37.

In the neighboring bed, Ethan remained fast asleep and snoring. The two had stayed up until well past midnight, drinking more than six beers apiece, along with the better part of a pint of whiskey Ethan had dug out of his suitcase. To the best of Chris's recollection, his friend's endless litany of stories about their youth had seemed not only bearable, but damn near entertaining the more drunk he'd become.

Which is probably why I was dreaming about Chicago, he thought. *And Dad.*

Limping to his feet, he shuffled into the bathroom. Planting one hand against the wall behind the toilet and holding his dick in the other, he pissed for what felt like an hour. After that, he found a four-cup coffee maker on the countertop by the vanity sink, but only decaffeinated packets to be made.

"Shit," he muttered, because if ever there had been a morning in which he needed a loaded cup of joe, it was that one. With a yawn and a scowl, he left Ethan sleeping in the room, and headed for the motel office in search of caffeine.

"Sorry, mister," the kid behind the front desk told him. "Just gave the last packet out about ten minutes ago."

Great. Chris resisted the urge to beat his forehead against the counter.

"You might try across the street at the RV campground," the kid suggested. "The guy who owns this place, that's his, too. They've probably got extra packs in the office. Just tell them you're staying here."

◆

Chris jogged across the highway, waiting long enough for a tractor trailer to barrel past, loaded with livestock, judging by the pungent stink of manure left in its wake. Wind from its passage buffeted him, rocking him back and forth.

It was early enough for most anyone with common sense to still be blissfully asleep, and thus, there was little activity in the campground. To his surprise, as he walked toward the office, he saw Bill and Libby Warner approaching from the opposite direction, both carrying towels and toiletries on their way to the bathhouse.

Shit, he thought, turning quickly and pretending to read the announcements on a nearby bulletin board. He doubted either of them would recognize him, especially in the dark, but decided not to take any chances. Out of the corner of his gaze, he watched the couple part at the bathhouse entrance, Bill for the men's side and Libby for the other, and once they had disappeared inside, Chris took off. His mission to find coffee forgotten, instead he retraced their steps in search of the old Winnebago. It didn't take him long to find it, much less to decide.

I'm going in there.

He knew Ethan would shit a brick if he found out, and if he'd been there with Chris, he'd have said he was nuts, but nonetheless, Chris was determined to try. All he could think of was Jessie, and how she'd looked at him in the diner with a sort of inexplicable but apparent distress.

She looked scared, like she was in trouble. I have to help her.

He paced a slow, cautious circle around the RV, pausing now and again to vainly peek in the windows. All of the curtains had been tightly drawn, and he glimpsed no hint of movement from inside, heard no noises — no TV, radio, nothing.

Sucking in a deep breath to steel himself, he reached up and caught the door handle in his hand. It was locked.

Now what? None of the windows had been open to his observation, not even a crack. The entire camper was sealed up tightly and the Warners would probably be back any second.

Not to mention Ethan's going to be waking up soon, wondering where in the hell I am.

Thinking of Ethan gave Chris an idea and he dipped his hand into his back pocket, pulling out his wallet.

Remember the time Mikey busted us into his uncle's house to get that fifth of Jack he swore was hidden underneath the kitchen sink? Using nothing but his goddamn driver's permit, you remember that?

Chris drew out his driver's license and stuck it between his teeth while he jammed the wallet back into his pocket. He'd never actually tried Mikey's lockpicking methods for himself, primarily because any time they'd needed them in his youth, Mikey had been around to employ them. It had never seemed too hard or taken too long, though, to the best of his recollection.

He jimmies it between the door and the jamb, Ethan had told him, and Chris shot a wary look around him, then, shoulders hunched to disguise what he was doing, slipped the edge of his license into the slim margin of space between the door and its frame.

Gives it a wiggle or two to wedge it underneath the bolt, Ethan had said, but Chris found it took at least five or six before he was able to get it into place.

Then he gives it a shake, Ethan had said, and Chris did this, counting softly to himself.

"Once, twice, three time's the charm," he whispered, and his eyes widened in surprise as he heard a distinctive *CLACK,* the door unlocking.

"I'll be goddamned," he whispered with a shaky laugh. *I owe you one, Mikey.*

He stepped inside the camper and found himself facing a small kitchenette. Fishing his phone from his pocket, he thumbed on the light, panning the dim beam slowly to gather his bearings. To his right, he saw a living room area and beyond it, the dashboard and driver's seat. An air freshener shaped like a cross dangled from the rearview mirror. On the left, a plastic, accordion-style door had been pulled shut, obscuring the rear sleeping compartment.

"Hello?" he called softly, hesitantly. "Jessie, are you in here?"

Nothing but silence in reply. The air felt thick and heavy inside the camper and had a strange odor about it, like maybe a mouse or something had died in one of the cupboards and started to rot.

"Jessie?" he tried again, but still no response.

Get out, he told himself. *Ethan was right. She's not here. You need to get out — right now.*

But then he thought of that little note, carefully folded and written in blood, begging for help, and the fear he'd seen in Jessie's eyes, and knew he couldn't. Not yet.

Not until I'm sure.

He pulled the accordion door back and looked inside the sleeping compartment. Here, a twin-sized mattress sat flush against the back wall of the camper, the rear window above it, curtains closed. He saw something in the bed, a small, shadow-draped figure.

"Jessie?" Seized with adrenaline, he hurried across the room, not knowing what he meant to do, maybe scoop her up in his arms and carry her out of there, back to the motel with him, like some kind of lame-ass hero in a cheesy movie. "Jessie," he began, reaching down. "Jessie, can you —"

His voice cut short when he touched her. Judging by how cold and stiff she felt, she'd been dead for at least the better part of the day, long enough for rigor mortis to have fully set in. As the light from his phone fell across her, he saw she'd been flayed, every discernable inch of her skin stripped away with gruesome, surgical precision, leaving only raw, glistening meat behind. Her eyes bulged from the confines of their lidless sockets, and because her lips had been cut away, her jaw hung lax and ajar as if frozen in a shriek.

Clapping his hand over his mouth, Chris felt his stomach gave a queasy lurch. "Oh, Jesus...!" he gulped, staggering backwards, floundering into what felt like a heavy curtain behind him. Not until he turned around, the phone light bobbing unsteadily in his hand, did he realize what it was.

Like a handwashed garment hung on a line to dry, Jessie's skin dangled from a series of hooks affixed into the camper ceiling. Everything somehow seemed to be intact, as if it been cut open along invisible seams, then peeled meticulously away from muscle and bone. Her limbs dangled down in lank, fleshy folds, her face toward the sagging remnants of her belly and breasts, her hair still affixed to her scalp.

Oh Jesus! Chris wheeled around and puked up the last of the previous night's overindulgence in beer. His phone tumbled from his hand, the light winking out, plunging him into darkness.

Oh, Jesus, he thought again in a terrified panic, reaching blindly for it, fumbling around on the floor. *Oh, Jesus, oh fuck oh HOLY FUCKING CHRIST these people are crazy! I have to get out of here! I have to —*

He heard the floor creak, and the snap of a switch, and suddenly, the back room of the Winnebago flooded with bright, fluorescent light. With a startled cry, Chris whirled, then backpedaled in stricken alarm.

"Well, look who it is, Bill," Libby Warner said, standing in the doorway beside her husband, smiling as if pleasantly surprised. "One of those nice boys from yesterday. I told you they were following us."

"How the hell did he get in?" Bill said, turning to shoot her an accusatory glare. "Did you forget to lock the door again?"

"Well, of course not," she replied. "You stood there and watched me—"

She uttered a yelp as Chris charged the doorway, knocking her aside and plowing Bill off his feet. As the old man crashed down onto his ass, Chris stumbled past, making a frantic break for the front door. Just as he reached for it, meaning to shove it open wide and run like hell, something slammed into him from behind, catching him between the shoulder blades. It felt like an arrow fired from a crossbow, striking hard and sinking deep, punching through vertebrae and severing his spinal cord in an instant. He felt his legs abruptly give out from under him and, like a marionette with its strings cut, he collapsed to the floor.

"Goddamn it, Libby," he heard Bill exclaim. "Why'd you do that?"

"I couldn't very well let him go, now could I?" she replied. "Besides, I have a new one, and now you do, too. We'll be a matching set."

Chris groaned, unable to move. Everything from that brutal point of impact in his back down felt leaden and numb. He managed to turn his head enough to look behind him, and by the light in the bedroom, he could see what had struck him: a long, spindly, articulated appendage that had burst from the base of Libby's right hand. She held her arm out toward Chris, with the skin of her wrist split in a wide gash, and that bizarre, bloody proboscis waggling in the open air between them like a grotesque extra limb.

"But I don't want this one," Bill said, sounding irritable. "I liked his friend better, the one who came up to us at the gas station."

"Beggars can't be choosers," Libby chided lightly. "He'll do just fine. Look how young he is." With a grunt, she yanked the protrusion loose from Chris's back, and it dangled, twitching, from her arm. "And so handsome, too."

"His friend was roomier," Bill complained. "You know I hate it when they ride up on me."

"Beggars can't be choosers," Libby told him again. "Why don't you at least try him on and see how he fits? If you still don't like him after that, I'll catch the other one for you."

Bill heaved a put-upon sigh. "Fine."

His entire face began to sag as, with a moist, squelching sound, he dragged it off like an ill-fitting rubber Halloween mask. What lay beneath wasn't even remotely human, but instead something monstrous, with black, glittering eyes and a gaping mouthful of jagged, pointed teeth.

Chris tried to scream but couldn't. "What…are you?" he moaned, as Libby lifted her arm, and with it, the whip-like length of bony protuberance from the floor. Now he could see the distal-most end of it, and the part that had struck him—a long, wicked spike, like the stinger on a scorpion's tail. As she leveled this at his head, drawing it back to strike, he clamped his eyes shut. "Oh...oh, Jesus...*what the fuck are you?*"

◆

By the time Ethan woke, it was nearly ten o'clock. He found himself alone in the motel room, much to his bewildered surprise, and after poking his head vainly into the bathroom, calling Chris's name, he wandered down to the office to search for him.

"I think he went across the street," the clerk said, pointing out the window. "He said he wanted to get some coffee."

"Huh." Ethan scratched his head, puzzled. "I guess I'll wait for him, then."

"Checkout's at eleven," the kid reminded as he walked toward the door.

"Guess I won't be waiting long," Ethan muttered in reply. Pulling out his cell phone, he sent a quick text to Chris: *Hey, dumbass, where are you? It's time to roll.*

He stopped at a soda machine to buy a can of Mountain Dew. As he cracked it open, he looked out toward the nearby ribbon of highway and watched a couple of tractor trailers go by. Beyond them, across the road, he saw an RV campground and, pulling out of the entrance, a familiar sight—that piece of shit Winnebago Chris had been going on about all yesterday afternoon. Although Ethan stood too far away to make out who might be behind the wheel, there was no mistaking either it or the ridiculous bumper sticker on the back: *HONK if you've been SAVED!*

As the camper drove past, he lifted his hand in greeting. He still didn't get why Chris had been so worked up. After all, the old folks driving it had seemed harmless enough.

Nice, even, he thought, looking down at his phone, waiting with mounting impatience for Chris to reply.

The Periphery People

"Yesterday upon the stair, I met a man who wasn't there," the man at the bar said to me, nursing a fresh two-fingers' worth of Ketel vodka in a tumbler he cradled between his thick, calloused fingers.

"'He wasn't there again today. Oh how I wish he'd go away,'" I answered, drawing his sleepy but surprised gaze from the basin of his drink. "*Antogonish* by William Hughes Mearns. That's what you were quoting right?"

He studied me for a moment as if seeing me for the first time and trying to size me up.

Most of the terminal drunks who typically dragged their sorry carcasses into the tavern this time of the night amused themselves by ogling my tits or hitting me with slurred promises of unimaginable sexual pleasure. Not this guy—John was his name. His first name anyway, or at least that's what he'd told me. I didn't know his last one, didn't really care.

When he said nothing, I rolled my eyes and turned away, grabbing beer mugs off a drying rack by the sink beneath the bar and mopping beads of residual water away with a hand towel.

"Forget it," I muttered. Why try to carry on an intelligent conversation—much less a literary one—with someone who'd pretty much polished off a fifth of vodka all on his own, all in less than two hours?

"What's your name?" he said.

"Mel," I replied. "Short for Melanie. No one calls me that except my dad."

He'd asked me this before and I'd answered him the same. I waited to see if there was any dawn of recognition in his face at the words, wasn't the least bit surprised when there wasn't.

"You drink, Meg?" he asked.

He'd called me Meg every time, too.

I held up the mug in one hand, the towel in the other, gave both demonstrative little shakes. "Not while I'm on duty."

I didn't tell him I never drank because my old man was a drunk, and even though he'd been clean and sober for seven years now, once upon a time, he'd liked to get into the Pabst Blue Ribbon and then slap me and my mother around for shits and grins. I had never tasted alcohol. I worked in the bar so I would never forget it—the hot stink of booze on his breath—and how much I hated him still for that.

John nodded once, fingered his glass again, and tossed back the entire dollop in a solitary swallow. "That's good," he told me, his gaze wandering distantly toward a nearby pale water ring stained into the top of the bar. "I wish I'd never started. Maybe then they'd leave me alone."

I glanced around the pub. It was a Tuesday, almost midnight—almost closing time.

Besides John on his bar stool perch before me, the place was pretty much empty. A couple of kids with greasy hair and too many crude tattoos to have earned them anyplace but prison loafed in a far corner, shooting pool and drinking beer. They had one girl between them, a bleach blonde in a too-tight denim miniskirt who didn't seem to mind the two-to-one odds.

Figuring what the fuck, I had nothing better to do, I took the bait and walked back over to John. He had that cast in his eyes, a tone in his voice that my chronic drunks sometimes affect when they want to get nostalgic or wax rhapsodical.

"Maybe who would leave you alone?" I asked. Probably his family—his old lady and kids. He was wearing a wedding ring. Old ladies, kids and chronic alcoholism seldom mixed company amicably.

He looked at me. "The periphery people."

I blinked at him, wondering if I'd heard him right. "The who?"

Still he studied me, his gaze unwavering—surprisingly steady, in fact, given the amount of booze he'd been knocking back that night.

"Periphery people," he said again, pronouncing the words slowly, carefully, as if each was a delicate crystal vase he was trying to swaddle in newspaper before packing away in a box in the attic. "Although they're not really people. Not like you and me. I don't know what the hell they are." He blinked, his eyes growing cloudy again, and he looked away. "Never mind. You can't see them."

Again because I had nothing better to do—and because I was actually caught off-guard by both his poem quotation and his use of a functional vocabulary word not typical of the common lexicon—I leaned comfortably across the bar. "Why can't I see them?"

"You have to be drunk," he replied. "Or at least I do anymore. Didn't use to. I could see them just fine on my own when I was a kid. I think kids are more receptive to seeing them. They believe in things, you know? Like Santa Claus or the Easter Bunny."

"Or periphery people," I supplied and he nodded. "The periphery of what?"

John flapped his hand, indicating the room. "Here. There. Everywhere. Everything. They're always around, standing in the shadows. All along the edges."

"The periphery," I said.

"Yeah." He lifted his glass to his lips, then realized he had no more vodka.

"So they're here right now?" As he set the glass down, I reached for the Ketel bottle and topped him off.

"Yeah." Nodding to me in thanks, he took a small sip, smacked his lips appreciatively and drank again.

"You said they weren't human. What do they look like?"

He shrugged. "They're tall. Really tall. Like seven or eight feet high. They wear cloaks, hooded cloaks. The cowls cover their heads."

Cloaks. Cowls. Periphery and poetry. I was beginning to wonder if this guy, John, wasn't your typical chronic drunk at all, but something more...tragic.

I made a show of glancing around, brows raised. There were plenty of shadow-draped edges and corners in the dump where I worked. Not a one of them seemed to be harboring a seven-foot-tall giant hooded man with a cowl over his face.

"You can't see them," he told me.

"Because I'm sober."

"Yeah. But they're hideous." He shuddered, though whether from this admittance or the drink, I wasn't sure. "Their faces are flat. There's nothing there — no eyes, no nose. Only a mouth. Round and gaping, taking up almost the whole front side. Ringed with teeth. God, lots and lots of teeth — rows of them going backward down their throats, just like a shark."

The color drained somewhat from his face, leaving him with a sort of putty-colored pallor. "They like to eat, you see."

Maybe it was the unspoken body language that seemed to suggest this poor son of a bitch was really buying the snow cone machine he was selling to the Eskimos. Whatever the reason, I found myself simply staring at him. And fighting the urge to shiver.

"Eat what?" I asked, my voice uncharacteristically small.

His expression shifted, growing grim, his eyes round and earnest. He whispered one word in reply to me: "Souls."

I'd expected him to say "human flesh. " Maybe even "brains," or perhaps spleen, appendix, right little toe. This, however, caught me by surprise.

"Souls?" I asked.

"They latch on to the back of your head with their teeth. Then they wrap themselves around you, make you carry them around like that while they glut themselves. Sometimes they take a little. Sometimes they take a lot.

Depends on how hungry they are." The cracked vinyl seat cover beneath his ass creaked as he shifted his weight, pivoting to glance behind them. With a nod, he pointed out the ménage-a-trois-in-situ playing pool. "You see that girl over there?"

"Yeah."

Turning in the seat again, he leaned across the bar toward me, close enough for me to smell the vodka in his breath. "One of them's feeding on her right now."

I took another look, but saw only the blonde laughing, slapping away one of the guy's hands as he tried clumsily, vainly to grope the generous outward swell of her ass.

"She looks okay to me," I said.

"Because you can't see it. And she can't feel it. Not yet anyway."

"But she will?"

John nodded. "One day, yeah. She'll find out she has cancer. Or AIDS. Or maybe she'll step off the curb at the wrong time and get plowed into by a bus. Or have a psychotic break and shove a seven-inch-long butcher knife through her husband's sternum while he's sleeping one night. But not at first. That comes later. I've seen it. No, at first...she'll just be sad."

"Sad." I repeated this, brow raised.

"You ever feel like everything in the world's gone wrong? Like you can't do anything right? Like the world is nothing but a big pile of dog shit, and you're just a smear in the fecal matter taking up space? That kind of sadness, that sort of despair—that's what they leave you with once they've eaten enough of your soul. From there, it only gets worse. Because that sorrow...that unhappiness, it must smell good to them, draw them somehow. They're always with you after that, like a pack of wolves, fighting over you, for their chance to latch onto your skull and drain you dry."

I've been tending bar for a long time—for seven years, starting about the time my mother had died and my dad had first sworn on her deathbed that he'd go clean, and then had shocked the glorious ever-living shit out of me by sticking to that. I've heard a lot of stories, yarns woven by a lot of guys far more wasted and crazy and pathetic than John. But for some reason, I couldn't just bob my head and cock that condescending smirk that I usually reserve for someone shitfaced and rambling. The in-one-ear-and-out-the-other look, I call it.

"They've fed from you, you know," he told me pointedly.

I felt a chill steal down my spine, slithering and unnerving, like a live eel dropped down the back of my T-shirt. Managing a hoarse bark of laughter, trying my damndest to sound dubious, I said, "What?"

He nodded.

"How can you tell?"

His eyes found mine—round, sorrowful, nearly sheepish. "You knew the poem. You haven't always been a bar maid."

Normally, that antiquated and decidedly misogynistic term—bar maid—might have made me bristle. But this time, instead, it only sent another of those unpleasant little tremors racing down from the nape of my neck toward my ass.

"No," I said in slow admittance. "I was a teacher. English literature. High school."

"World civilization," he said by way of introducing himself in ex-career fellowship. "At the university. Had tenure and everything."

We studied each other for a long, quiet moment.

"Something happened," he said. "Something that changed you. Maybe a moment you can't quite put your finger on or remember, but it's there. And in that moment, whether you knew it or not, a part of your soul was gone."

"My mother died," I said. "My dad's on disability. He can't get around. I have to be home in the daytime with him. There's no one else who can take care of him."

"Feels like your life's being sucked right out of you sometimes, doesn't it?" John asked, and when I nodded, hesitant, the corners of his mouth hooked in a brief, bitter smile. "Because it is." A glance beyond my shoulder, split second but pointed. "There's one behind you right now."

I whirled, eyes wide, but saw only rows of liquor bottles and phalanxes of cocktail glasses lined up dutifully along the shelves.

"It's not feeding," he continued. "Not yet anyway. But it wants to. And there's only one way to stop it."

"How?" I asked. As ridiculous as this whole thing sounded, I couldn't help but believe him. There was such a tremendous, sorrowful sincerity in his face, his eyes. It was as if all of the booze had been wiped from his system and he was sober again—brutally, helplessly so.

He leaned toward me. "You have to see them. " His hand draped against mine, his skin dry and warm. "If you can see them, they'll leave you alone. " Another fleeting, humorless smirk. "No sport in it for them then."

As he drew back his hand, he shifted on his stool again, letting his feet fall heavily to the floor. I shook my head as if snapping out of a trance. For the first time, I realized we were alone in the bar. The trio of pool players— along with their invisible, soul-sucking new friend—had left.

"You ever see movement out of the corner of your eye?" John asked, fishing his wallet from his back pocket and dropping a pair of twenties onto the bar. His glass still had vodka in it, but he left it alone, turning with a shuffling gait for the door. "A flash of shadow, maybe, like something's there, just beyond your field of sight—only when you turn your head, it's gone?"

I nodded and he said, "That's them. The periphery people."

He started to walk away, but paused when I said, "What about you? You said something changed me—the moment where one of these things fed from me. What about your moment? What changed you?"

He looked over his shoulder at me and this time when he smiled, it was something melancholy and lonely. His lips pursed, then parted, as if he meant to speak, but then he must have thought better of it because he closed them again. Still shuffling, the palsied gait of a man far older than his years, John turned again and walked away, leaving the bar without another word.

I locked up behind him, the heavy sound of the deadbolt sliding home as I turned the key as sharp and loud as a gunshot. I tried to laugh it off, to tell myself he was just a crazy drunk, that he'd been spewing vodka-infused bullshit he wouldn't even remember come the morning.

But then, as I started to turn away from the door to face the bar again, I thought I caught a glimpse of something reflected in the glass—a looming shadow directly behind me, standing just along the peripheral edge of my vision. With a startled gasp, my heart jackhammering in sudden, bright fear, I whirled around, pressing myself back into the door. I was alone. At least, to my sober eye.

There's one behind you right now, he'd told me. *It's not feeding, not yet anyway. But it wants to.*

I thought of how he'd described them—their ghoulish mouths ringed with teeth so they could latch on and hold tight. Again, I wanted to dismiss it—and him—as utter bullshit, and again, I couldn't suppress an uneasy shiver just the same.

There's only one way to stop it, John had told me. *You have to see them.*

I returned to the bar and stood beside the seat he'd only recently vacated. His last shot of Ketel remained where he'd left it, and I reached for it now, lifting the glass in hand, giving it an experimental sniff. I'd never tried vodka before; had felt neither the urge nor desire to drink myself into a stupor.

If you can see them, they'll leave you alone. No sport in it for them then.

Bracing myself, I drew the glass to my lips, tossed my head back and swallowed. Having drained it dry, I leaned forward, poured another and downed it. Then a third. Then a fourth. And after the fifth, as my mind started to grow murky, and the shadows in every corner of the room seemed to grow elongated and sinister somehow before my eyes — becoming nearly human in shape, creeping closer to me, slowly but surely — I took a seat on the bar stool.

And waited to see.

About The Author

S.E. Howard lives in Kentucky where she works as a registered nurse, certified in toxicology (a fitting field given her side-hustle writing horror stories). Her short stories have appeared in numerous anthologies, including *PUSH! An Anthology of Childbirth Horror* presented by Ruth Anna Evans, *Carnival of Horror* from Undertaker Books, and the Amber, Sinister, and Green Diamond Editions of *The Horror Collection* by KJK Publishing. Her short story "You've Been Saved" was also adapted for the screen in the 2022 GenreBlast film anthology *Worst Laid Plans.* Her horror novella, "Prairie Madness" is available from Baynam Books Press, and a novel, *The Vessel* from Wicked House Publishing. For more information, visit online at www.sehoward.com.

Acknowledgements

The Bobbit was first published in *Nothing Ever Happens in Fox Hollow, Volume 2: A Horror Short Story Anthology*, edited by Richard Kodai (December 10, 2021).

Swan Song was first published in *Hotel Evil: Vacancies: 13*, edited by Chisto Healy (Black Ink Fiction, April 13, 2021).

The Stranger was originally distributed as exclusive to subscribers for Wicked House Publishing's Patreon, August 2025.

The Baxter Family's Quantum Vacation was originally edited by Chisto Healy. Based on characters created by Chisto Healy, for an untitled anthology project in 2021. The publisher for this project went defunct, and the idea was shelved. I'm so happy to bring it, and Chisto's wonderful Baxter family, to readers. Used with his permission.

The Devil You Know was first published in *Wicked Universe: A Wicked House Publishing Anthology*, edited by Cassandra O'Sullivan Sachar (Wicked House Publishing, December 20, 2024).

It Will Have Blood was first published in *The Horror Collection: Amber Edition*, edited by Kevin J. Kennedy (KJK Publishing, May 11, 2025).

You've Been Saved was first published in *Worst Laid Plans: An Anthology of Vacation Horror*, edited by Samantha Kolesnik (Grindhouse Press, July 1, 2020).

The Periphery People first appeared October 19, 2014 on Creepypasta.com, written under the name Sara Reinke.

Made in the USA
Middletown, DE
19 November 2025

22096655R00126